For Pat and Polly,
long of the departmental
family

STOWAWAY

STOWAWAY

a novel by

LAWRENCE SARGENT HALL

An Atlantic Monthly Press Book

Little, Brown and Company

BOSTON   TORONTO

ATLANTIC–LITTLE, BROWN BOOKS
ARE PUBLISHED BY
LITTLE, BROWN AND COMPANY
IN ASSOCIATION WITH
THE ATLANTIC MONTHLY PRESS

*Published simultaneously in Canada
by Little, Brown & Company (Canada) Limited*

PRINTED IN THE UNITED STATES OF AMERICA

STOWAWAY

To C. R. L.

for supplying many strands

1

THE LAST I ever heard of the *Liberty Belle,* which was our name for the old rustbucket, I actually overheard by accident one rainy afternoon in a dingy steamship office in Sydney, Australia, where I was waiting to have cleared up some paper difficulty in connection with my transfer to a new billet. I was anxious about the difficulty. I had originally meant to leave the merchant service once the war was over, when by one of those strokes of luck that catch you off guard I was offered a third mate's job — my first. I seized the opportunity not from ambition but as you would take advantage of a sudden windfall that gave you an unexpected chance to pay off a rankling debt, to settle a score.

The nature of the irregularity in my papers was beyond me — one of those recondite technicalities quite alien to the understanding of the person to whom it applies, on which nevertheless his participation in the affairs of the human race hangs. Nor would anyone in authority explain the trouble to me, whether because I was incapable of comprehending or because it was none of my business, or both, I did not know. All I knew was that it existed, though not from any fault of mine or of anyone else so far as I could determine, that it must be dealt with, could only be dealt with officially through channels. Like entering a hospital — it was my body and my ailment, but they pre-empted, they owned them.

The steamship office was dreary, a rectangular space with no more decoration than you might expect to find in a warehouse. In spite of its being early afternoon the bare bulbs gave off a sad yellow light over row upon row of desks which stretched from wall to wall like bunks in a barracks. Seated at the desks strewn with piles of papers in various stages of processing between trays marked INCOMING and other trays marked OUTGOING, or crisscrossing busily up and down the aisles with documents in triplicate and quadruplicate fluttering from their carbon-stained fingers were pale clerks, assistants, agents, and what not, most of them wearing glasses that glinted cold and efficient in the unflattering light. Behind the subdued drone of many voices, all converging to the same pitch and timbre, punctuated by the ringing of bells and buzzers, could be heard the incessant chatter of typewriters and business machines translating the raucous, unwieldy physical activity of men, vessels, and cargo into the forms and symbols of commerce. Compared with this spectacle the sweating of stevedores, screeching of winches, swinging of cranes, pounding of engines, whirlwinds, fogs, seasickness, sinkings, drownings, bravery, cowardice, skill and duty — all the live conditions of hurling tonnage by the millions around the watery globe — seemed as remote as a game of chess being played by mail.

The clerk who was handling my problem had disappeared in search of some mystic protocol or sanction that would put my future in order on paper. Sitting there like a mere article of business I was attacked by a twinge of alarm at the realization that this sober, officious, unimaginative, callow little man, who had never been afloat in his life except in a skiff among lily pads, was manipulating my career in his perfunctory hands with no more sense of what it meant, where it

4

had started, what it had been, how it would end, than the typewriter on his unattended desk.

I gazed around me at the indifferent bustle, which appeared to be without origin or conclusion or any tangible achievement beyond an uninterrupted routine flux of paper, and was seized by a nightmarish fancy that I was a bystander observing the rarefied process of fatality, whereby the facts of life were administered by statistical cause and effect that had no palpable connection with them. All these functionaries, apparently abstracted from reality — unless in fact this was reality and everything else was not — were collaborating in loading commodities they had never used, aboard vessels they had never seen, dispatching them in the charge of men they did not know, to ports they had never visited, without any idea how they got there, why they were sent, what became of them — and without the least interest in these solid matters, or what was worse in their own part in them.

While I awaited in some trepidation the return of the expert of my particular destiny, the door of the glass cubicle next to the desk where I was sitting swung open and one of the higher officials, the purity of whose decisions required isolation, paused in the doorway giving to his secretary the instructions which I overheard.

"Oh —" he said, "and if you have time, make out papers transferring that Liberty ship number so-and-so. I've forgotten the number but it's there on the form —"

He hung in the door. I heard his secretary call off a number, like a croupier, and my brain rouletted. It was the *Belle's* number, and it affected me like the unexpected recurrence of a fever.

"Yes —" corroborated the official, his hand on the glass knob, "that's the one. Let's get it out of the way. Transfer to such-and-such. The name is around somewhere. It may be that Greek outfit. About all she's good for is scrap." He started to pull the door to and stopped. "Oh, yes, and one more thing. Notify Freemantle. They're probably still hold-

5

ing her on their books. They'll be glad to strike her off. Send them a copy of the transfer for their files. As of such-and-such a date —"

Then and there, with the shutting of that glass door, the old *Belle* — the unwanted statistic, the unremembered number on a half-remembered docket — received her final dispatch into the files and her account was closed. It was so simple it was shattering!

My callow little lubber of a factotum returned, handed me my documents with an official smirk, and announced pontifically, "There — you are all taken care of. Everything is in order."

Once upon a time I had hated his kind for the casual power they wielded over you. My peculiar humor had always been a calculated individuality, a sense of myself, I suppose you might say, as a phenomenon not unlike other men yet not the same, as if from the primordial slime to the twentieth century the chemical components of organic nature acting out their incorrigible laws had produced in my case something a little special and therefore free. I could not see myself "in order," so to speak, being "taken care of" by some incredible rule.

This is why, when the war broke in upon my preserve, I did all I could against being inducted into the highly-regimented nonsense of strictly military organization. It was not easy, since I had rejected both dependency and dependents. I had only my mother, old and ailing, but financially secure through my father's estate. I had even considered the way of the conscientious objectors until I saw it followed an orthodoxy I could not subscribe to. That left as my most likely course the merchant marine. I had spent two years as a merchant seaman after college, partly to see the world but largely because in the midst of my senior honors work, to the bafflement and dismay of my professors, I was literally horror-struck by the sudden terrible vision of myself and all my classmates, there and everywhere, not merely that year but all years, docilely forming up and falling in with the inexorable procedures, like sheep into the fold, like rookies to the drill hall. The thought of society marching me with every other down its formal corridors swept me as with a fear of life imprisonment. So I packed my books and clothes, and on a milk train at two o'clock one morning took flight as desperately as any escaping convict, and went to sea on a cattle boat.

In view of these things I was rather surprised at myself, receiving from the stubby tarnished fingers of this authoritative clerk the documents that put me in order and took care of me, accepting at face value his statement (which was extravagant to say the least) that I was *all* taken care of and that *everything* was in order, feeling a pleasant glow half of comradeship half of security, and finding myself before I quite realized it thanking him cordially, gratefully, for picking me up, for doing me a service, a favor, in fact a saving grace.

I left him with the impression of his cold dry hand in my palm, and wended a way down the aisles past the desks of all the other clerks who cooperated it now seemed in the vast benevolent enterprise of caring for me and keeping me in good order. Outside, while I waited in the doorway for a heavy shower to subside into the more regular drizzle of the day, I puzzled over this new-found happiness. I felt a trifle guilty for it. I threaded back through my interview to the beginning and retraced each detail and nuance to the end. I worried it without enlightenment until I remembered the part about the *Belle*. It could simply have been relief that the system which had eschewed that ignominious vagrant forever had, at least for the nonce, revealed a willingness to do otherwise with me. What it had done with the rest, my shipmates, I did not know. I could have found out, and I may say it was not any trouble it would have required which deterred me. As a matter of fact, there was no need of knowing. If they were obscured in deepening shadow, what was

7

lost? Our point of reference was the *Belle*, and all that remained must be seen in its afterglow, as all that preceded was reflected from it as by a mirror.

Rain or no rain I decided to have a last look at the *Belle* if I could find where she lay tied up. I had only the most general sense of where this could be. I might have gone back into the office and inquired, and I briefly considered doing so. They would have appreciated what they would have taken to be my sentiment. Though it was not sentiment, I would have been unable to explain it as anything else. So, since I did not like the falseness of passing it off as that, and since the patterns of coincidence seemed charmed in my favor for the moment, I set out through the soft rain, thrusting my papers crackling down as far as they would go in my pocket, more or less to follow my nose.

2

I FOUND the derelict moored alongside an unused dock in the silent company of several other dilapidated rejects — a collier, a cattle boat, and three or four hogged scows and barges. Her armament had been removed from her decks, her lifeboats from their davits, including, I at once observed, the one which had harbored my discreteness. Her holds and tanks empty she sat high and shabby and quiet like an old floating rubbish pail. Not even the rain gave her any polish streaming down her soiled sides. Her portholes were lackluster and she was stained overall with the dull grimy reddish hue of corrosion. The never-ending task of preservation and cosmetizing had been abandoned altogether, and imperceptibly, as I watched, the slow secret rust born of her very vitals was spreading unchecked through and through her.

From everything I could see and everything I could hear, the last amounted only to the diminishing splattering raindrops — the water was as grayly, stagnantly still as the land around, I was in a morgue literally enough, and any undertaker would have joined me in dismay that the cadavers were not decently laid out.

Not only was the old *Belle* not going home to die, the re-

9

mains were not even being shipped back. An ancient carrion, she was going to extinction far from her origins, on the other side of the earth from the New England yard that she rose in. The dissolution that was inherent in her metal, that had begun even before she was framed out, awaited only the irresistible acetylene. The transformation from welding torch to cutting torch, from keelblocks to scrap heap, was almost complete. Whole, she was worthless.

I stood for several minutes depressed. No one, not so much as a dirty half-drunk caretaker moved about. I had wanted to find the *Belle* by myself, look finally on her and leave her — by myself. And there I was, and the dead ship, like the curiously impersonal corpse of an abandoned mistress, woke old, intimate, guilty virilities and lusts.

She sat so high that the bottom of her accommodation ladder hung suspended above the dock out of reach. I had not intended to go aboard, there was no point in it. But I had not expected the ladder would be rigged. It was not too far overhead for me to jump and catch hold of. I glanced round to make sure no one was there to see me, sprang, pulled myself up, and stood on the bottom step almost against my will. The ladder shuddered alarmingly. It occurred to me that I might be in trouble if caught where I had no business being, and this gave me a sense of squalid adventure as though I were scaling the wall of a ramshackle building by a back-alley fire escape. As I climbed, the rust ran across my hands and over my wrists like dried blood washing away. To keep it from staining the sleeves of my raincoat I kept trying to push them up without touching them with my fingers, by rubbing them together along my arms.

From the main deck I had my choice of entering the sailors' quarters which lay along the starboard side of the deckhouse, or climbing the ladder outside to the boat deck. I stood there quite a while unable to make up my mind, not that the decision was in the least important except in the fact that it had to be made. I finally chose the ladder.

10

As I opened the after door of the deckhouse I felt like a man who has made a serious mistake. My error seemed implicit in the deathly vacancy and silence — the rain had stopped — all about me: in the grotesquely wilted davits — what use could they have for those old lifeboats — in the doors to the chief mate's and the third mate's rooms, which I could see standing open to provide a gray shadow of light at the forward end of the passageway. I hated to shut myself into this dim vacuity, but someone passing along the dock might notice the open door.

It was like entering a crypt or a mausoleum. To my right as I lay forward the steward's room and the hospital were closed. I was tempted to try them to see if they were locked, but proceeded on instead. At the end of the passageway I saw that the second mate's and chief engineer's doors were open, as well as the mate's and the third's, so that had it not been that the only remaining furnishings were desks and chairs askew, bunks without mattresses, half-open lockers, and in the mate's and chief's room each a metal filing cabinet, I could have presumed all officers had precipitately abandoned ship in some abortive emergency, leaving their doors ajar.

Annoyed and a little intimidated, as if it were a kind of sacrilege, by the resounding of my heels on the steel plates, I paused at the turn of the passageway and found myself gazing directly into the mate's old room, with a graphic recollection of the familiar pictures which had once covered the wall above his desk. They had been taken in some gymnasium in South Boston and showed O'Hara and his cronies, wearing boxing gloves and trunks, in all the poses and attitudes of The Pugilist. O'Hara had, in fact, been good enough to get almost up to the big time, and proud enough to quit when he saw he would never really make it. He did not have the temperament to be a second-rater. Simms, the third, a Midwesterner ten years his junior, used to spar with him on deck with twelve-ounce gloves in calm and cool weather.

11

But Simms, a third-rater by design, could never take it seriously enough to let O'Hara teach him, and this perplexed O'Hara, who could not understand how a man was able to enjoy getting himself consistently walloped. He was a sportsman's sportsman and for this reason, in spite of a quick temper and a streak of rather mystical perfectionism, he had got along well during the war with officers and men, including the Old Man, who also respected him and more than O'Hara, being a South Boston Irishman, was inclined to believe of a skipper who came from Harpswell, Maine, whose grandfather had been a prosperous master builder of Cape Horners, the topmasts of which the Old Man's father had stood many times around the world. The Old Man himself had been until retirement before the war master of one of the niftiest small luxury liners in the American merchant marine.

Left on the bulkhead now were only the tiny squares and rectangles of color in various sizes which the pictures had protected while the paint faded unnoticed around them. I moved on past the door of the second mate, Sayles, a dry, leathery Alabaman ten years O'Hara's senior, faithful and always complaining — about the food, about the war, the men, the work, the weather, the strictness of Yankee skippers whose forebears had first got rich shipping Negro slaves into the Southland and then got richer fighting to free them.

The corner room on the port side had been occupied by Chief Engineer Costello, from New Haven, who liked silk shirts and silk underwear — "It gets sticky as a salt mine in that jesusly engine room!" I could almost hear the echo of his resonant bellow whenever the mate teased him about his "wop finery." He had a voice of remarkable quality and timbre, which he exercised freely, especially to drown out with flamboyant Italian arias the sentimental Irish tunes O'Hara would offend him by crooning one after another all day long from an inexhaustible repertoire. "Drooling," Costello had called it, and he would burst into the midst of

O'Hara's coming back to Erin with turning to Sorrento. It was a queer battle of music between the Gaelic ballads of a wind-blasted northern island and the Latin lyrics of a sunny Mediterranean peninsula, and as often as not it was routed eventually by the bawdy ditties interposed by Simms in his Midwesterner's twang or the revivalist meeting hymns wailed out by Sayles in his Southern drawl. To Simms's ditties, which seemed to be inspired by a curiously concordant and international motive, the other three ultimately yielded as to a basic harmony that either transcended or subsumed the most profound cultural distinctions.

In those days I had a habit of speculating on the unknown wasted potential, the hidden talent, the secret virtue — as well as vice — that is never found out because no one really looks for it, and my speculation about Costello was that he would have made a great opera singer but for the accidental ignorance and indifference of himself and people around him. The gift of a Caruso may not be the rare phenomenon it is assumed to be at all; without the fortuitous combination of circumstances, temperament, intelligence, and will to reveal and develop it, many an engineer, chef, or lumberjack may go to his grave with as rare a gift, and the world, you might say, none the wiser but much the poorer, if that means anything.

So Costello, sweating it out below decks with his magnificent voice bawling orders into the din of machinery, might have been a famous operatic tenor if he, if somebody, had known or cared. Instead, there he had been, a damned good engineer. Even in ten-knot convoys (which was close to our maximum) we fell behind only once, and we never had been obliged to drop out as many a better vessel had. There he was, I say, in his machinery spaces more immaculate than any mess hall, Costello — the Wop, in silk underwear, liking his job, his women, his liquor, hot Italian sauces, our repulsive steward because he was something of an expert in these last, and the Old Man and O'Hara because their incomparable shiphandling saved him from answering bells. Once after O'Hara had made a one-bell landing, light, and had tied up to a tanker for fueling, in a nasty tidal eddy where the tanker was fighting her mooring like a hooked fish, Costello had appeared in the wheelhouse and said to the Old Man: "I'll push steam for you on any ocean if it is in a pisspot." The Old Man merely nodded his stupendous head in the direction of O'Hara. Costello said, "You do that — you redheaded mick?" And the mate said: "No thanks to you. She's got so much freeboard from you not ballasting tanks I had to *sail* her alongside."

This was a remarkable feeling for Costello to express, accustomed as he was to regard everybody above decks as passengers. He was a great union man. He believed devoutly in the brotherhood of engineers, which somehow presumed the hostility and knavery, if not the outright idiocy, of all who were not members of its technological fraternity. It was a closed society, and Costello ran it like an elegant overlord, a king ruling a tight little empire. He had almost as much power aboard as the Old Man, and anyone else, including O'Hara, had to treat him with the utmost tact and respect. But he was worth it. You got the same impression of most merchant vessels, where the master's success with the company in keeping to schedule absolutely depended on his engineering officer and therefore on his relations with his engineering officer. Temperamentally and by virtue of his position Costello, who might have been an opera star, was still a genuine *prima donna*, and was able to command the treatment of one. Topside personnel took the engineers at their own valuation, and regarded them circumspectly as a special breed of cats — of pasty, nocturnal, somewhat fanatical cats. So that there were times when the ship seemed to be not an organic unity at all, but two separate entities, made up of her conn on the one hand and the machinery on the other, and held together in careful truce through a delicate bilateral treaty between the brain and bowels.

14

I climbed the ladder to the bridge deck thinking sadly of these men — the Mick, the Reb, the Wop, they had amicably called each other. Accident had tossed them together and in spite of their differences in background, in personality, in religion, in prejudice and purpose, they had once made a team together, and individually, I reflected, they had also done notable things. Staring down the passageway, which disappeared in a tunnel of darkness before it got to the Old Man's door, the lock of which I did not have any desire to test, I began to review some of these things, wondering how much they had been forced by that iron spirit with its invincible illusion, and how much by the pressure of common risks and common action.

I glanced once into the radio shack, emptied of its gear, and suppressed with a shiver the memory of Sparks, the radio operator, a frail studious man who had seemed to be made unremittingly nervous by the gap between his scientific inclinations and his meager education; he had stacked three whole shelves with books on electronics and had pored stupefied over them for months, with his long stringy hair straggling every way around his narrow head and his grimy fingernails bitten bleeding to their quicks.

Then I thrust aside the thought of his dreadful recourse and entered the wheelhouse. Here I had been more at home than in my bunk, and for longer than I had in my lifeboat, and my recollections echoed succinctly among the silent fixtures.

3

THE DAY was brightening slowly as I gazed down
through the narrow ports onto the bow I had for so
long watched thrusting its ponderous, turgid way through
countless miles of sea. There is a vast undefined promise in
the bows of any craft, however ungainly and ruthlessly practical they may be, from the snub-nosed punt to the racy,
spritted clipper. As a solitary boy I used to lie in the stern
of my sailing dory, the tiller against my shoulder, while the
sheering gunwale tilted and dipped against the open curve
of vacant ocean, or against on another tack islands or main-
land, low-lying and secreted in shade, fresh and hazy blue as
unmade history.

In the transcendent, timeless sunshine you were as good as
a Viking, a John Smith, a Hendrick Hudson, seeing these
sparkling waters and this shaded land for the first time, entering unexplored channels and strange coves, searching for
gunkholes along kaleidoscopic shores. A pointing bow, even
the stubby, graceless bow of the *Belle*, is a probe of the
universe of sea and sky across which one day falls the blue
shadow of your promised land. Somewhere, I once dreamed,
there would be in the south seas, in the north seas, east or
west of wherever I was, a turreted island or a continent, a

city, a race of men with the climate and life to suit me. I did not have to accept what I had, I could wait. And as the flaring bow of my dory grated on the sand of some secluded haven, so huger bows — even blunt, stolid ones like the *Belle's* — would someday discover my special paradise.

But as I stepped back from my vista out the ports and went to lean my forearms on the wheel, the fact I had to lament was that these bows had not been the *Belle's*, at least not hers. Hers had merely grounded out at the last on the shifting sands of my memory.

I gazed about me. I had stood hundreds, maybe thousands, of hours on watch in this wheelhouse, marking the bow cleave water, daylight, darkness; steering assigned courses reflexively so that I had also stood watch among my ideas. Every scratch on the varnished wheel and in the paint on the bronze binnacle was familiar to me. And what had occurred on these watches I found I remembered with brilliant clarity and the instantaneousness of a dream, against the slow stillness and the dust.

I remembered one storm of near hurricane velocity, force-ten wind and sea, when the bosun was swept overboard. He and the third, Mr. Simms, were in charge of a working party on the forepeak trying to make fast one of the forward booms which had broken loose in the seaway. It was not an uncommon accident in conditions like the existing ones, but it was the first time it had happened to the *Belle*.

The ship had been wallowing since daybreak, rolling sluggishly like a sick leviathan so that I was lucky if I kept her within five degrees either side of course. She was carrying about ten degrees of right rudder all the time, with an impossible tendency to fall off to port, the way a vehicle gets sucked deeper and deeper aside in snow or muck with every foot of progress. Half an hour at the wheel was enough to exhaust the stoutest helmsman. She took an interminable while to respond, and once she started we had to roll that wheel with all we had to meet her before she got away from us to starboard. It was like sliding sidewise down the whole earth. The seas would crash staggeringly against her side and explode, throwing huge jets of spray and green water over her bridge. "Choppy," the Old Man said, bracing his immense old body against the wheelhouse after bulkhead. Mr. Sayles, the second, worriedly suggested turning tail and running before it, but the Old Man ignored him and held his course. He was not one to deviate readily, and whenever he was obliged to he seized the earliest possible opportunity to get back on course.

When the steel vang snapped like a violin string as the boom swept across deck to leeward, we could feel it in our feet like a minor seismic shock in the wheelhouse. "Number one's starboard boom has let go!" Sayles shrieked. And the Old Man roared, "Head her up — hold her into it. Mr. Sayles, notify Mr. Simms to get the bosun and a working party on the fo'c'sle — with lifejackets!"

Heading into the eye of the wind reduced our roll, but there was still enough action to send the boom slamming to port and fetching up with a colossal shiver to starboard. Jets of water spouted through the hawsepipes, shot into the air over the bulwarks, cascaded off hatches, ran in freshets past coamings, sluiced athwartships trapped in black eddies by the rolling deck, in a slithering rush for liberty squirted through the scuppers on the low side and poured foaming back into the sea.

The broken vang swung in mad hyperbolas through the air so that the men stumbled in arcs like drunken Maypolers trying to catch it and at the same time avoid having their skulls bashed in. It was almost comical to see their clumsy antics before the fiendish intelligence with which the broken fitting that weighted the end of the cable alternately eluded their groping arms and took homicidal aim at their heads. At length the vang made a wide evasive sweep and wound itself in accelerating coils around the mast, where the end struck viciously like the head of a snake and fell off listless.

Bohunicky, our bosun, pronounced Bonicky, called Bo-hunky or the Bohunk by his friends, shinnied up the mast with the agility of the gorilla he resembled, fastened a piece of rigging through the fitting, dropped apelike to the deck, unwound the cable and tried to take it to the boom. For the next few minutes, as the boom crashed back and forth across the deck, he was yanked about dangerously close, sometimes towed on his knees, sometimes on his belly, sometimes on his back, but always in various fighting postures of trying to regain his feet in those brief instants when the boom hesi-tated. Holding the rope's bitter end he waited his chance, and the instant the boom came to starboard got a couple round turns on the bitts, where he was joined in a flash by several others. He was working to take up slack when a forag-ing, omnivorous gray lip of the sea swelled over the forward chocks and swallowed the entire fo'c'sle. When it drained away aft it left the men skipping and dragging from the vang like half-drowned mackerel on a troll line — all, that was, except Bohunicky, who had vanished into the ravenous watery maw.

"Stop engine —" roared the Old Man above the gale. "Come hard right!"

As the *Belle* veered, procrastinating, and finally hove to, what happened on the forward deck in the next hour ap-peared from the wheelhouse a pantomime. In response to the gesticulations of Mr. Simms one man struggled up the mast, bulky as a beetle in his lifejacket. The others clung along the bulwark searching the sea to leeward.

Following the Old Man out onto the starboard wing the second wailed, "Cain't lower a boat in this!"

For all his raw muscularity — he could take his two hun-dred and twenty pounds up a rope hand over hand with the wild speed and ease of a monkey — the Bohunk could not swim. He had grown up landlocked among the coal mines of West Virginia, moved on in his teens to the steel mills of Pennsylvania and Ohio, and finally joined the merchant

19

marine because he thought he was going crazy from the darkness and noise. On a ship he could have sunlight and silence while at the same time feeling the vibration of machinery and the touch of steel. He loved to work. He was respected by the officers because, prodigious in his own energy, he could drive his men to exhaustion if necessary, and by the men because of his strength and a vilely devastating humor. "Whatsamatter, Rose —" he would bellow at one of his fagged-out, drooping deck apes, "you got the curse?" Whereupon the man would fall-to as if the curse of curses was to shirk from labor in the Bohunk's sight. Nobody tangled with Bohunicky, but nobody really wanted to.

The odd thing was, he seemed to have brought his darkness with him. It became intensified rather than dissipated by the contrast of life on the weather decks. Though he fitted the appearance and possessed the attributes to perfection — all, that is, except the ability to swim — he was never meant to be a bosun. He discovered that in reality he feared and hated the water, disliked the wind in his face and the sun in his abnormally protruding and vulnerable gray eyes. Off duty he took to hanging out below with the black gang, and worked for a while to be one of them. But in spite of a brute wit and wisdom, incomparable agility, a sense of crude mechanical advantage, his aptitude was fundamentally one of bone and muscle, and even the *Belle's* old-fashioned reciprocating engine was a miracle of incomprehensible device to which he was fated to listen in worshipful ignorance. Nevertheless, of what he had he gave without stint, and what he was called upon to do he did obdurately and with incorrigible heart. All that can finally be said of better men could have been said of him. He was needed.

In this instance, while he floated somewhere off our lee bow in the element he so abhorred, O'Hara, striding angrily out onto the wing, indulged in what for him was a rare piece of sentiment. "I'd risk the boats and half the crew," he growled, "for that Bonicky."

Down on the forward deck, while the *Belle* rolled sluggishly broadside in a lather of foam along her flanks, the man on the mast presently waved his arm, pointing abeam. The Bohunk was sighted. Intermittently he showed atop those crests which rose higher than the others, and as suddenly and suspensefully disappeared in the troughs. He was flailing desperately, trying to paddle back against the driving, intolerable wind and water, encumbered by his lifejacket. But it soon became obvious that the ship was drifting toward him too slowly, and buoyed up as he was by that lifejacket he was being carried away in spite of his efforts, a little farther at each appearance.

Here it was that Mr. Simms threw off his own lifejacket, as a couple of men whom he had previously dispatched returned with a coil of rope, secured the rope around his waist and dived forthwith over the lee side. He made no splash of his own, and it was several seconds before he was spotted. He was a strong swimmer who could in calm water be seen to surge with power. But in that tossing sea his dark perishable head, more often than not submerged, seemed a ridiculously frail vessel on which to stake a life. Most of the way he was hidden from view as the men on deck payed out the line, a slender, all but invisible thread from where I was. These motions beside the bulwark in the protracted, anxious intervals of Simms's disappearance were the only evidence that he lived and strove. It took him nine minutes down wind to reach the bosun and, after we had finally caught his signal from the summit of a wave, it was thirty-two minutes before the men hauling in the rope dragged them both aboard. The second mate had frantically, pointlessly clocked it all.

From the wheelhouse we saw them surrounded by the others while head down on hands and knees they vomited the salt water they had taken in. The Old Man ordered the *Belle* headed up. Meanwhile, kneeling and gesticulating, Simms and the Bohunk, shouting soundless orders to the men, directed the final securing of the boom. The slack and snapping vang tautened, the boom was winched off the deck, the men swayed in unison on a jury-rigged guy, the mate and bosun knelt, with opening mouths, and the boom fell into place. When the job was accomplished and the boom stowed once more, all disappeared like puppets from a stage.

The Old Man said: "Half ahead, Mr. Sayles — make your course." And as he started away to his stateroom he added, "I've seen worse storms, but never seas so sharp. It's the shallow water."

Later the Old Man called the steward and ordered Bohunicky and Simms into the saloon. While they were sitting there in dry clothes and the steward was pouring them coffee the Old Man strode in, set a fifth of Haig & Haig Pinchbottle on the table, said shortly, "I suggest you kill this," turned his high angular back on the amazed faces of the third and the bosun, and strode out. He had the occasional custom of inviting the two ensigns, our gunnery and communications officers, to his room for a drink, but he never drank with his own officers, or with his men. And life or death made no exception to his rules.

That was the extent of his unbending in this instance, and if it appears casual it was more than matched by Simms and Bohunicky. Once the Old Man had made his official exit Simms said to the steward, "Uncork this and get us a couple glasses and a deck of cards." They sat there for two hours getting drunk and playing twenty-one until the bottle was empty. After which they simply went to bed.

It was all in the line of work, part of their common lot. No one ever heard either of them comment on the episode. And while it would have stuck in my memory anyway, what brought it to mind that rainy afternoon in Sydney along with rival episodes was a confusing change in attitude. I at one time had thought it was so significant a thing to save a life.

4

CAN IT be said of courage and heroism that they are like Costello's tenor — a raw gift which may either be ignored and squandered or cultivated and perfected? If there is value in human performance, what is meant by the nonchalance, the prodigality that takes it for granted, takes it as a matter of course, of life, and takes life that way as well? Takes, anyone must admit, weakness and vice and death, also capable of perfection, in the same way. How many men have succeeded not from plan, or even from desire, but because circumstances and their own flaws as well as strengths just happened to coincide in such combination that they were helpless to do otherwise? Or similarly failed? Moreover, how many virtues have proved shortcomings in certain conditions, and how many shortcomings virtues? Why put a premium on one and not the other? Why not perfect either, or both . . . ?

Of all the *Belle's* complement — they numbered about eighty — you would have picked Sayles, the second, and a second-rater all round, as least likely to be decorated for exceptional initiative in combat. He was over age in his job, partly from fear of any greater responsibilities, partly because of his record. He had started his career twenty years before the war on tankers. But he became a "sniffer." He had acquired an incurable addiction to inhaling the intoxicating fumes from the tanks of gasoline and kerosene, and while he might go along for months sober, struggling, his guts aseethe with the terrible craving, his whole consciousness centered on it, he never knew when he would succumb. But at length he always hopelessly knew he would.

On frequent occasions he had been dragged away in the nick of time, half dead, and still he found it impossible to resist, every second of every waking hour, the dark infernal peace of the lapse, the giving in, the giving up. Once he went for fourteen months and five days, by his scrupulous count, and then just as he thought he might have kicked the habit they gathered him up from a vent pipe or a hatch, limp as an oily rag, his eyes rolled back into his head, their corneas gleaming like eggs, the crud-eating smirk of the sniffer on his deathly face, and lugged him to the hospital.

This cruel phenomenon of himself so frightened him that he finally fled the tankers for good, and did not go aboard them even to visit any of his old shipmates. "I'm a sniffer," he would explain with scientific fundamentalism, much as a man might say, "I'm tone-deaf," or, "I'm a bleeder."

There was a certain condescension in his attitude to men who, never having been singled out for real temptation, were therefore unable to be really virtuous. He regarded his sniffing as a kind of fraternal emblem. He felt himself a member of a vast congregation of unfortunates composed of fellow sniffers, of alcoholics, of murderers, of various less elite backsliders, who even unreformed and unregenerate were yet the only ones capable of appreciating the full meaning of rectitude. His addiction was to him a sign of something so basic to the impenetrable scheme of things that it could only be referred to sacramentally. He offered it as evidence of his personal share in mankind's original sin, and his virtue as well as his pride lay in atoning for it by a self-lacerating preoccu-

24

pation with the most trivial details of duty, a self-righteous, fanatical, and usually crippling fussiness.

Off duty he read and reread illustrated editions of quasi-religious tracts, the most dogeared one of which I remembered was entitled *Love Our Benighted Brethren*. And love them he did, with a complacency so helpless that it had in it something that was both wistful and appalling.

It seemed rather ironic that he should hold the Silver Star for an impractical and untoward act which in the excitement of the moment he hardly knew he was committing. Even this act, as he construed it, had something to do with his syndrome. He had simply been unable to help himself.

The event occurred during the Anzio operation. We were hove to, part of a task force screened from aerial attack by a dense pall of smoke that drifted slowly over us from pots which the escort vessels had launched a mile or two to windward. Flash-red alerts had been coming with regularity all the previous day and night and all this day, keeping us sleepless and on edge so that we belched continually. Borne on the light breeze, as if the smoldering fires of hell had been fanned up, the smoke came sifting on us so dense and acrid occasionally that topside we were seized with paroxysms of sneezing.

"Like being home — achew!" the navy ensign who was our gunnery officer observed, "in good old Pittsburgh. Achew. . . ! I love it —" He belched. The smog which he once must have deprecated now wafted over us like a mantle for whose filmy protection we were all inordinately grateful.

Between belching and sneezing the navy gun crews manned our guns, though they had orders not to give away our position by firing. Most of the planes we heard droning at a distance, carrying out uncertain and sporadic bombardment or strafing wherever they could find a target, but now and then one or two passed with a roar, close yet invisible, overhead.

It could not have been more than two or three minutes

after the steward had poured everyone coffee on the bridge that we heard several planes coming toward us in a great crescendo. Deafened by sound and blinded with smoke, we stood still as wax, each man with a white half-empty coffee mug in his hand. Then the din was on us and in us. One plane passed down our starboard side, an owl-like shadow in the foggy dusk, no farther than twenty-five yards out, flying low.

"He's spotted us!" yelled the gunnery officer. "Hold fire!" The starboard twenty-millimeter gun crew tracked the fleeting shadow through its quick transit but did not shoot. We had scarcely time to separate the noise of the first plane from that of the second when the gunnery officer screamed — "Hit the deck!"

With a shattering blast of exhaust and machine-gun fire the monstrous shadow of the second plane flashed over us from stem to stern. When we looked around we saw two of the starboard gun crew curled up against the side of the tub as though they had fallen asleep from exhaustion. Very slowly the man at the gun began to move toward the deck. The gun was partially elevated, and as his knees bent under him both arms began slowly to rise above his head, not reaching but as if in supplication. He remained on his knees several seconds and then, his arms slipping through the shoulder harness, rolled quietly over on the deck.

What Sayles then did he did so quickly that it registered on none of us until well after it was done. He leaped upon the gun, not bothering to shoulder the harness. We heard him scream in a voice of frenzied rage, "Yew dirty bastards . . . !" And he commenced firing. At nothing at all. Round and round in circles into the obscure smoke the fiery tracers streamed out targetless like fireworks from a Roman candle, not in bursts but in steady wild and aimless flight. All at once there was a lurid flash, a thunderous concussion as if the air had blown asunder splintering the farthest silences of space, and the voice of the gunnery officer screaming, "Cease fire — cease fire! You fool — goddammit, cease fire!"

Sayles dropped the gun as quickly as he had fallen upon it, and in the smoky stillness stepped back over the body of the gunner and looked dazedly at us.

Tense and frightfully alert we froze in expectation of the attack the exploding plane, betraying our location, was sure to bring. In our positions, arrested in the attitude each man was caught in at the instant of the explosion, we resembled figures in a museum. The Old Man towered grimly, his head turned to starboard while his body faced dead ahead. The navy communications officer, an ensign just out of college, crouched at the top of the ladder, his torso twisted as though he had been about to bolt below. The gunnery officer's mouth remained sagging open behind the mouthpiece of his headphones. He still held his coffee mug, as the Old Man and O'Hara did, but most of the others were scattered about the deck where they rolled placidly. Time took on dimensions once again, measured by the roar of planes receding astern and diminishing finally in the heavenly distance. Sayles, confronting us, let fall his hands which he had held spread palms out as though in startled apology. The communications officer licked his lips into bright pink.

"Jesus H. Christ —" exclaimed the gunnery officer — "he got one! Scratch one and he never saw it. My God!"

Sayles was standing spellbound. Tears, the combined result of exhaustion and shock, begun to roll down his narrow cheeks.

"Mr. Sayles." The Old Man stirred authoritatively. "Will you pull yourself together or leave the bridge?"

Ludicrously Sayles put his hands over his ears and nodded between them.

"Lay below a while. Send some men to remove the bodies," the Old Man told him.

It had been against orders, it had jeopardized our lives, it had been a fantastic coincidence, but Sayles had indisputably shot down an enemy aircraft and the gunnery officer was

27

obliged to report the incident. This he did. His report was picked up at a moment when the navy had issued a directive to improve by any means available the touchy relations between its personnel aboard merchantmen and the regular crews. Accordingly the task group commander recommended Sayles for a decoration for avenging the deaths of three navy gunners.

Sayles received it awkwardly and tearfully in a brief ceremony in which all aboard participated, in full uniform, with sarcastic and grumbling good will. All, that is, save O'Hara, who in protest against the dazzling irrationality of the whole affair kept to his stateroom. The citation was read by the Commodore's chief-of-staff, and the Old Man in his impressive, deep-boweled voice responded by delivering a simple eulogy of the navy gunners who had died at their unfired gun in the strict line of duty. Afterward there was a lot of good-humored joking about Sayles's marksmanship. The communications officer, who was something of an artist, painted in cerise which he lovingly mixed from odds and ends a hash mark and a set of wings on our stack — a device that immediately became known as "Sayles's Angel."

None of this altered Sayles, or his own or anyone's estimate of him. He continued to go about wearing his expression of perpetual dismay. He simply remained Sayles, the plodding, fretful second who had chanced to get himself a medal for doing because he was rattled what not even he would have expected him to do, and what in truth he should not have done anyway.

There appeared to be no agency in the actual deed, and therefore no basis for appraising it beyond the mere fact that an enemy plane had been providentially or accidentally, depending on how you looked at it, shot down. Unless — and this was the puzzling thing — you interpreted it to be evidence in Sayles of an original virtue, uncontrolled and dangerous in exactly the same way as the vice of sniffing fumes from the tanks.

28

5

NOW O'HARA would never have acted so. He had a habit of guiding himself in any situation by a severe and often jesuitical logic. This got him a name for being harsh and unfeeling, "a hard man to shave" as the bosun put it, and those who could not understand the impersonality and abstractness of his position considered him self-righteous. To give him his due you had to admit he was under no delusion as to his infallibility; as a matter of fact he blamed himself for his failures more inflexibly than he blamed others for theirs. Still it had to be said that he was sweepingly intolerant of anything unreasonable or unsuccessful, and he tended to equate the two.

He had real intellectual power, the sort of power that responsibility requires, but that also requires responsibility — the sort of power that does not make a man popular and does make him more than a little feared. His logic was uncompromisingly functional. Bedeviled by it himself he bedeviled others with it. To a lookout who had fallen asleep on watch and pleaded that he hadn't meant to, he said, "What the hell has that got to do with it? It's what you do, not what you mean to do, that keeps a ship afloat. So you sink us all — I suppose we should think nothing of it because you didn't mean to."

After the ceremony honoring Sayles's heroic exploit, and the navy four-striper had left the ship, O'Hara stalked into the Old Man's stateroom. Simms and the bosun and I happened to be in the chartroom when he went by. He closed the Old Man's door, but it failed to latch and fell ajar just enough for us to hear him say, stiff and formal, "Skipper, I want to recommend the transfer and replacement of the second mate."

After a pause the Old Man's voice boomed, "On what grounds, Mr. O'Hara?"

"For his bungling which might have lost us the ship, and may yet."

The Old Man took a little longer this time before he said, "Mr. O'Hara, a good officer is a hard-nosed officer. But that officer needs to remind himself from time to time that the world is full of people who are not hard-nosed, and he has got to live with them. We are all in this together, Mr. O'Hara, and there is more to each of us than his efficiency or limitations."

O'Hara apparently made a move to interrupt, for the Old Man said, strengthening his voice, "Just a minute." He paused. "A man stretches himself — or you stretch him — for all he's worth. That may not be enough. But it's as far as any of us can go, except for one more step — learning to get along with our limits. The secret of command, Mr. O'Hara, is to get out of a man what he's got to give. This is the best Mr. Sayles, or you, or I would take elsewhere and the best a replacement would bring aboard here."

"I don't particularly like kicking him down the ladder," O'Hara protested. "But it's this ship that's to be taken into account, not some other and not Sayles. It's tough, but it goes with the job. He's got his Silver Star, and other ships expect to take care of themselves."

As I listened I reflected — both these men had the fundamental prerequisite of survival: they were tough, tough for life and tough for death. But at the same time they were a stalemate of affinity and antipathy.

The Old Man said, "The group is made up of the individuals in it, Mr. O'Hara. If the individual is damaged the group is contaminated. You can't escape that. Fidelity to duty is all you can demand. And that is in the heart. Efficiency is in the head and comes second."

"Do I understand," O'Hara asked in a legalistic tone, "if the ship is sunk because of keeping Sayles you would say that is preferable to sacking him and saving it?"

"All I ask," the Old Man responded heavily, "is that he does his best and does his duty. The rest is not in my authority."

O'Hara's athletic intelligence went for the opening. He said, "That's what I'm saying. Your authority is confined to this ship. If you've got no ship, you and all the rest of us including Sayles have got nothing."

With finality in the trailing off of his voice the Old Man replied, "I did not put Mr. Sayles aboard here. You operate within your jurisdiction and prerogative, Mr. O'Hara. There are some things that are worse than nothing. When you attempt to operate beyond your jurisdiction and prerogative, that's what you get. You have my attitude. That will be all."

In the dead silence which followed, O'Hara's voice, curt with repressed argument, sounded the formula. "Aye, sir," it said, and without another word he emerged from the Old Man's room and returned to his own.

The bosun said to Simms and me, "See the backs of his shoes?"

"What about the backs of his shoes?" Simms asked.

"He shines 'em," Bohunicky said.

"So what?" inquired Simms.

Regarding Simms with his protruding eyes Bohunicky announced: "An officer don't shine the backs of his shoes don't wipe his ass."

31

Simms snorted, and twisting his neck and shoulders scrutinized his own heels. "Not too bad," he said, amused. "Not good, but not bad." He started away.

Following him Bohunicky observed blandly, "The backs of Mr. Sayles's shoes is never polished."

Yet, of the behavior I could recall of the three mates, Sayles's celebrated shot, wildly coincidental as it was, seemed in a certain respect the purest of all in that it was a wholly spontaneous outbreak of his undeliberate self.

Hearing at this time the Old Man get up and close his door upon the departure of his chief mate I dwelt on their conversation with an uncomfortable mind. The thought of making a choice between them dismayed me, but the natures of both were enunciated so positively as to seem to require that a choice be made, and even then I knew if pressed, as I somehow felt I was, I would have to take the Old Man. What is more, I was morally certain that if O'Hara had been obliged to choose a skipper other than himself he would have been willing to settle for Captain Blake.

I remembered distinctly his action one night returning to the ship on a late liberty launch, when the first junior officer of a converted troop transport was obliged to give seating preference to the Old Man. The officer was noticeably drunk and disgruntled. He gave way, but as the Old Man sat down beside him he said in a surly manner, "What grave did they dig you out of, Captain?"

The Old Man ignored the sneer, but O'Hara, who was standing in front of the officer with his legs apart, balancing himself against the light motion of the launch, glared coldly down at him. Holding to his perfectionism even in drink, O'Hara deemed it a requirement of superiority to carry undetectably a quantity of alcohol sufficient to paralyze an ordinary man.

"What's your experience, Captain — tramps?" the officer persisted.

Still the Old Man ignored him, and O'Hara glared.

The officer, sourly aware that his face could now be saved only if he got the Old Man to lose the dignity of his silence, tried again to break through. "What is your present command, Captain — some Liberty also ready for the graveyard?"

Suddenly O'Hara, swaying with the roll of the launch in the darkness, snapped, "You got the wrong man, mate!"

The officer, his great bulk outlined and his heavy features lit palely by the running light, gazed upward at O'Hara. "Who'd you suggest I get?" he inquired truculently. "You?"

"I suggest you pipe down," O'Hara said, very cold.

"That's enough, Mr. O'Hara," the Old Man rumbled, his eyes never straying from their original focus midway between O'Hara's belt and his chest.

"That's too much, Mr. O'Hara —" the officer said, lumbering to his feet before O'Hara. "How's if you pipe down?" Then he swung his right arm at O'Hara's middle.

O'Hara twisted so the blow glanced off him, and as the officer staggered there off balance in the heat of the night and of alcohol, O'Hara hit him niftily, twice in the stomach doubling him over and three times in the face straightening him up. Then he grappled with him to throw him over the side.

The coxswain rang his bell, the engineer threw his engine out of gear, and the launch coasted softly, losing way on the black still water.

O'Hara had the huge officer with his waist on the gunwale, too stunned to struggle seriously, when the Old Man rose and called in a formal voice, "Desist, Mr. O'Hara." Reaching out his long arm he hauled his mate back by the shoulder while the officer rolled round and lay with the small of his back against the gunwale, the blood pouring darkly from his nose.

The Old Man, confronting O'Hara, growled almost pleasantly, "I am above the need of this."

33

Restraining his breath O'Hara said, "I am not." He bit it off.

"That will do," the Old Man insisted in a fatherly tone. "No more." He resumed his seat.

The coxswain, reassured, rang his bell, the engineer engaged the clutch, opened the throttle as the bell rang again, and the launch having lost little headway picked up her speed once more. Turning his back the officer leaned on the gunwale with one elbow and got out his handkerchief. Physically he was not much damaged. But clearly he was demoralized by the sanguinary efficiency which had disposed of the physical prowess he was used to counting on.

O'Hara took up his former position in front of the Old Man and remained there staring out into the night over the Old Man's head until the launch came alongside the *Belle's* lighted accommodation ladder.

As the Old Man was disembarking the officer stepped over to him, still holding his bloody handkerchief, and said soberly, "I'm sorry, Captain." The Old Man nodded and put his hand kindly on the officer's shoulder to help himself over the gunwale. To O'Hara the officer said with a mixture of admiration and remorse, "I should have known better."

"Skip it," O'Hara said. "I'm a pro, I shouldn't have hit you."

Once on his own deck the Old Man said, "It would do you good, Mr. O'Hara, to make a mistake yourself now and then."

"I do," O'Hara retorted. "But not if I can help it."

And the Old Man, calling O'Hara by his first name for the only time in anyone else's hearing, said, "I never had a son. But if I had I think he might have felt called upon to do what you did under the circumstances." He carefully observed O'Hara flinch and avert his face. "And I think I would have felt called upon to reprimand him for it." Then, moving off, he added over his shoulder, "We're under way in the morning at oh-six-hundred."

34

"Aye," O'Hara responded. The Old Man went up to his room and O'Hara lit a cigarette with a tight little smile on his lips.

I wondered then, and I will always wonder, if O'Hara had fought out of respect for the Old Man, or for the Old Man's prestige out of his own self-respect as his first officer, or both.

6

O'HARA'S position aboard the *Belle* was difficult for him. He was overqualified for it. His nature and abilities were not merely suited for command, they needed it. But his luck had not been good. His aptitude for conditions that were challenging made him chafe, and in their absence chafe others. Skippers who had turned to him in trouble and been spectacularly bailed out turned resentful when they were out of trouble, which in O'Hara's perversely uneventful career was most of the time.

His whole character was attuned to, was constructed for, extraordinary circumstances, for the hazardous, and his ironic fate was to be dealt the routine lot which most men needed to escape failure, but from which he needed to escape to avoid it. The capability and quality of the man seemed created for emergency. Given a situation that would crush most men he would have thrived, but in the long tedious grind where success was established by careful, patient, conventional service, through the innocuous arithmetical qualifications of seniority, he wore his restraints away. Waiting was his crucible; it eviscerated and consumed him.

The Old Man had known this, and because he valued

O'Hara he had used his considerable influence to try to get him a ship of his own. "You keep a first-rate man back," he once admitted, "and not only the man but everybody is going to have trouble." The Old Man was secure enough in his professional supremacy not to feel threatened by O'Hara, as lesser skippers of O'Hara had. Yet he gave him even less responsibility aboard than they had because O'Hara was young, and the Old Man was bent on proving at the age of seventy-some that he still inherited the seas and required no brash youngsters to take over merely because a few cells were beginning to deteriorate and slow down his organism.

Worn hulk of a mariner though he was he had managed to get himself out of mothballs in the first desperate days of the convoys when experienced masters were at a premium. The war, it appeared, had been a godsend to him, for he had discovered during the enforced retirement from which it had rescued him that to relax in the slightest degree his tenacious grip on the world was to start the irretrievable descent out of it. Retired he was of no consequence. And he was not ready for that.

O'Hara was not in himself a menace to the Old Man; the menace was greater than that, was in fact inescapable, and consisted of the brutal axiom, which O'Hara just happened to personify, that as the young man's powers wax the old man's conversely must wane. O'Hara, on the other hand, had been young enough to believe still in the myth of his personal indestructibility.

Probably, even if the Old Man had given him part of the skipper's load, that would not have done. Being allowed to perform the master's duties is not the same as being the master. The core, the inspiration — knowing it is your ship and you are yourself the final authority, the last recourse, the only appeal — is missing.

While I remained in the wheelhouse of the rejected *Belle*, in full command by default of a deserted bridge O'Hara had never quite been master on, I felt his ghost most palpably of

37

all except the Old Man's. They had been, both of them, remarkable men, but each in a very different way. It was not merely that one was a South Boston renegade Irish Catholic and the other a Down-East Episcopalian patrician. It was a matter of generation, of era. O'Hara's generation could no more have produced Captain Blake than the captain's could have produced his mate. Blake, for example, would have gone down with his ship by instinct, being convinced of the sacramental value of this act of devotion to himself, his ship, and his seaman's code. It was good and meaningful in itself. O'Hara was equally capable of going down with his, but only because he had rationalized it as a legalistic necessity. Judging humanity and its deeds as he did, without reference to the infinite spectrum of personality, he could not have distinguished between these two actions because the results, you see — the results were practically identical. Whether they were enjoined by faith or by contract, actuated through ritual or calculation, they were both one in the end. To him both were essentially one from the beginning, though if he had thought about it, as you were sure the Old Man had, he would probably have denounced the way of faith as less viable.

The source of O'Hara's power was rational, of the captain's, moral. The strength of the young man seemed to derive from sinew, mind, and will, of the old man from marrow, heart, and spirit. You might count on either one, though I came sorrowfully to learn that neither was without his daedal and implicit flaw. You would probably have worshiped the Old Man, as I did, for struggling to keep alive all by himself in one sorely beset corner of civilization unfaltering fidelities, for their own sake, of a bygone age.

O'Hara, too, had put up his doomed struggle, for a rationally strict, almost classical order, where all had to be definitive and nothing could be left loose, unaccounted for, or alone — for a pattern of efficacy which gave him no room to make allowances. Where most men found discomfort in stringency, he found it in laxity. There were no Irish pennants dangling untidily within his purview. Between master and mate a kind of mutual respect without much compatibility served almost to the end as a basis of their relation. I recalled a graphic instance of the impasse of their personalities, where the Old Man's sovereign conscience was set off against O'Hara's jealous sense of form.

We were steaming one evening off the west coast of Africa in a ten-knot convoy, which was fast for us even in our better days. Our station was behind the lead ship in the fifth column, and the interval between ships was close at a thousand yards. As darkness fell the ships of the formation — tankers, freighters, and their slim anti-submarine escorts slithering back and forth like lean dogs herding sheep — dotted with their black silhouettes the smooth sea in all directions to the round horizon. The cloud of night was suddenly on us, and from the darkened ships and the darkened sky there was not a glimmer to prove we were not absolutely alone in a gulf of space. Only the feathery pips of light swimming on the radarscope like a school of phosphorescent sardines assured us electronically that we were in company.

O'Hara was standing his watch on the flying bridge, keeping station on the ship ahead, which he could not see, by ranges and bearings I called out to him. Our radar was outmoded and cranky, but we were fortunate to have any at all. The dimensions of the whole blacked-out world in which we moved existed exclusively on the little bright dial before me, and in O'Hara's blinded head topside.

Marked only by the quiet exchange of orders and data between me and the bridge, the bridge and the helmsman, this locked-up introverted watch was half over when all at once the darkness outside condensed, liquefied, and precipitated itself on the steel plates of our decks with the sound of a billion distant drums. I had never known such a rain. Inside of thirty seconds the port and starboard lookouts stumbled into the faint glow of the wheelhouse simultaneously, their clothes black with rain, their heads lowered, dashing the water from their eyes as though they were emerging from a nocturnal dive. There was no wind. The rain simply dropped oceanically and burst upon our plates. Milky mists like nebulae wafted across the radarscope. Sea return — rain return!

"Can't keep your eyelids open out there," sputtered one of the lookouts, wiping his face with his hands. "Christ — might as well be sinking!"

I expected O'Hara to appear momentarily in the wheel-house, but he did not. His preference for standing watches by himself was certainly strong.

The voice radio began to hiss. A metallic voice broke through the static. "All ships! All ships! Emergency course change to port — seventy degrees from base course! Emergency course change seventy degrees to port! Stand by to execute. . . ."

The lookouts ceased slapping at their drenched and cling-ing clothes and stared blankly in the direction of the speaker on the bulkhead. I hung in the doorway of the charthouse. For a moment the only things tumbling through my mind were the academic thoughts that emergency maneuvers were not executive, were executed upon the order, without stand-by, that still I wasn't sure, that perhaps the size and speed of the convoy, the closeness of the formation, the radical change of course in worse than zero visibility caused some-body — the commodore, the officer in tactical command — to modify the procedure so as in some way to reduce the great danger of collision.

Into the silence of the voice tube I shouted, "All ships — from convoy commodore — emergency course change to port seventy degrees from base course! Stand by — stand by to execute. . . ."

For several seconds O'Hara did not answer. In the wheel-house, breathlessly quiet against the drumming night, I visu-alized him up there soaking in rain and this sudden perverse problem. Our escorts must have picked up a submarine contact. I was on the verge of repeating the order, thinking he might not have heard it in the din and thickness of the rain, when his voice echoed humid and hollow as through a drain pipe. "Seventy degrees left of base course," he precisely acknowledged.

"Present course zero-three-three. Base course zero-two-five," I heard myself shout back.

"Radar —" he said into the tube, "I know the courses."

"Aye, sir," I replied.

"Range and bearing of the ship ahead."

I dialed the radar. "Range about eleven-hundred. Maybe a little under. Reception is not good. Can't call it too accurately. Bearing zero-three-three." O'Hara was a meticulous station-keeper.

"Stand by to give me ranges and bearings every thirty seconds after order to execute."

"Ranges and bearings every thirty seconds after execute."

O'Hara's orders were plain, thrifty, and formal, and he insisted as a precaution against failure in communications on hearing them acknowledged in terms of their information. Unlike the other two mates he was a stickler for procedure. I wondered what he thought about the standby execution of an emergency maneuver. Since he did not remark on it perhaps he understood it to be sound.

"Helmsman —"

"Wheel aye," I heard the helmsman sing out from the wheelhouse.

"What is your heading?"

"Heading zero-three-three-and-a-half."

"Make no errors to the left," O'Hara ordered.

"No errors to the left."

I called into the tube, "Shall I notify the skipper, Mr. O'Hara?" The question was routine in all unscheduled course changes. This time, however, it seemed to have special significance partly because after many hours on the bridge the

41

Old Man had retired not feeling well, and partly I must admit because, though I did not in the least doubt O'Hara's brilliance, I would simply in so risky a situation have felt better — not necessarily safer — with the Old Man up there.

Again several seconds elapsed, so that I was about to repeat when I was jolted to hear O'Hara say flatly and positively, "Negative."

He gave no explanation of this unwonted refusal, though clearly he had taken a moment to consider it. His policy was never to explain what was not necessary to your function, even if that left you asking yourself nervously, as I did in this instance, what he could have in mind. Why was he, stickler for formality as he was, deliberately leaving the Old Man unaware of this crisis?

My anxiety and suspense were tangible in my cold and crawling skin. And I realized that I was disquieted not by the navigational hazard or any doubt of O'Hara's ability to cope with it, but by that very ability itself; his intimidating readiness to close with the danger seemed curiously inhuman. What I feared was the threat of both the man and the problem locked in their unbenevolent geometry.

A minute perhaps, no more, had slipped by since the emergency command had crashed into the security of the watch's routine, when the radio hissed once again and the distant voice crackled electrically into the dense calm. "Stand by —"

"Stand —" my own voice cracked, "by —"

"Ready below —" O'Hara's words echoed damply back.

"Execute — execute!" The command fell upon the hovering instant like the signal to a firing squad.

"Execute — execute!" I beseeched.

"Execute," came O'Hara's neutral voice as from a disembodied intellect. "Steady as you go, helmsman," he called into the wheelhouse through the voice tube.

"Steady on," the helmsman sang against the drumming rain.

42

I punched the stopwatch hanging from the console before me and yearned upon the radar. "Bearing zero-three-three . . . range eleven-double-oh."

"Zero-three-three — eleven-double-oh." O'Hara above, seeing nothing, neither ships, his own bow, nor instruments, not even his watch, must be counting to himself, keeping time by speech, talking off the sceonds — one-one-thousand — two-one-thousand — three-one-thousand. . . .

It would be like hearing train wheels, or sitting in a rocking chair. But it connected him vitally with the facts of the night, which in the distillation of this Euclidean moment became purified into theory and existed only in his mind as in the mind of God.

Somewhere eleven hundred yards ahead the guide ship in our column on the order to cxccute had put her rudder over left standard, leaving an infinitesimal swirl of water about twenty feet in diameter in the inscrutable sea. All told there would be eleven such mathematical points in a line at right angles to her course — providing the lead ships of the other ten columns had been on station and applied rudder at the crucial instant. Theoretically the one hundred and sixty-five vessels following them would without eyesight locate these pivot points, apply left standard rudder at the exact second they passed through them, and turn together as if at the edge of the earth and the brink of chaos. . . . Thirty-thousand —

"Bearing zero-three-zero — drawing left . . . range one-oh-five-oh — closing." Eerie streamers of luminous cloud scudded over the school of pips on the radarscope. Prayerfully, despising the primitiveness of our radar — how I would have felt without any at all did not occur to me at the time — I said into the tube, "Reception poor but holding, sir. Data normally inaccurate under nine-hundred yards — contact usually lost at seven-hundred." It was a miserably narrow margin.

The voice of O'Hara said, "I know the gear. Give me your

best estimates and let me know when you lose contact."

Any ship turning too soon risked collision with the one ahead and the one to port, too late with the one behind and the one to starboard. O'Hara now had less than two-and-one-half minutes in which to find in the darkness of his brain the indispensable glimpse. The ship astern less than five-and-a-half. So it would be through eleven columns sixteen ships long. Millions of tons of dry cargo and explosives moving at a rate of better than three hundred yards a minute, requiring unknown hundreds of yards to turn and still more to stop, not even mechanical vision under seven hundred yards, eleven little vortices eddying in thousands of square miles of black sea, each vessel with its peculiar variable in human and mechanical reaction. . . . The probability of disorder virtually killed thought. One man making one mistake could set off the chain of contingency so that the enclaves maintained by each individual ship and each individual column would lose the distinctiveness of their organization and dissolve into the equality and sameness of chaos. It required a miracle of cybernetics. . . . Practically it was impossible!

Sixty-thousand. . . . "Bearing constant at zero-three-zero —" Too close — her stern was swinging in the night and she was not getting out of our way! "Range eight-five-oh — closing fast!" Less than two minutes to our vortex. . . .

"Give me a mark at seven hundred yards or, if she fades, the last range and bearings you get." He had something worked out for seven hundred yards, when he would have to extend the barely established pattern into sheer conjecture, and wait for the awful moment of proof.

My fingers trembled on the knobs and my eyes were watering. If she had lagged in turning we would hit her if we turned on time. I made a frantic resolution to call the Old Man, but was impotent to act on it.

"Lost contact! Just over seven-hundred — bearing zero-two-nine. . . ." We were off the edge.

"Time —" O'Hara's voice perfunctorily called down.

44

I focused on the jerking hand on the white-faced watch. "One minute thirty-eight seconds!" Had she turned late or early or on time? How many yards would she forge before completing her swing? What could O'Hara know?

"Range and bearing on number sixteen."

I seized the knobs. The forward pips had begun to scatter. "Sixteen bears zero-four-seven — range . . . about nine-five-oh." Number sixteen was the lead ship in the column on our starboard hand. If our guide had turned late and we turned on time we would hit him; if we turned in his wake, that is late also, number sixteen would hit us. If . . . the variety of combinations leading to disaster were staggering! I had begun to feel the close drumming of the rain as though it were inside my head.

"Give me a bearing on sixteen at eight hundred yards."

"Sixteen at eight hundred." How was he going to translate all these shifting figures of our relative movement toward other ships into a workably accurate braille with one long sightless minute still to go, project in his mind the reality not merely of this second but of the critical sixty seconds from now? Once upon a time I had witnessed a professed clairvoyant, his eyes bandaged on stage, describing the hiding places of lost objects and the future events in people's lives. I had credited none of it.

"Lost contact with sixteen at seven-nine-oh, bearing zero-four-five. . . ."

From here on O'Hara was on his own. The ranges and bearings from whose rough initial drifts he had had to draw his final exquisite perspective and make his final unalterable decision would during the last minute be running wildly in the dark. I sagged back in a vertiginous sweat feeling as though I had leaped over a precipice and everything was left to gravity and chance.

"Give me a mark at three minutes —" His remarkable perfunctory tone had not changed.

"Three minutes — aye." He had drawn his picture and

made his estimate. There was no way of checking, no basis for amending it. We had only to follow it out and wait for the inevitable reckoning. What did he know — how much had he wildly guessed at? Where had he put his trust, if any? He didn't believe in the Jesus factor. My eyes were on the dial of the watch. The school of pips on the scope was now unrecognizably distorted. The fine hand of the watch was sweeping our event to its conclusion. "Stand by —" I said, hearing my voice strangely clear and steady.

"Stand by your helm," O'Hara called into the tube to the wheelhouse.

"Wheel aye — standing by!" chanted the helmsman. The coincidental rhyme made him sound ecstatic.

"Look smart."

"Smartly —" the helmsman responded.

"Mark!" I shouted. "Three minutes!" Our correct interval was up. The subsequent pause was interminable and intolerable. Was O'Hara counting off additional seconds? It did not occur to me to call them out myself unbidden into this deadly silence. Had he panicked, unable to bring himself in the end to give the momentous command? Without calculating, as if it no longer mattered, I watched the sweep hand hitching through the first quadrant. Could he have fainted from tension, or dropped dead up there in the black rain? I was on my feet in a fury for the Old Man, knowing I would be too late, that whatever it turned out to be we were now enthrallingly committed to it.

"Left standard," O'Hara called through the wheelhouse tube at last, with a calm so godlike that my knees gave way. "New course three-two-seven." The last was a precaution in case something actually did happen to him before he had conned the helmsman to our new heading.

"Left standard —" the helmsman answered back.

"Call off your head at zero-three-zero and every ten degrees. We're heading for home!"

"Yes, sir —" the helmsman said, startled by O'Hara's

implication and warm tone. "Zero-three-zero and every ten degrees. Rudder is left standard."

Outside the rain drummed, inside the engine throbbed. The silence held.

"Passing zero-three-zero." The *Belle* had started her blind yawing swing.

"Passing zero-two-zero."

The sweep hand flicked around.

"Passing zero-one-zero."

The radarscope looked like a skillet full of scrambled eggs. I could not imagine what might be going through O'Hara's mind silently waiting out the invisible. I found myself spastically gripping the rounds of my stool, bracing myself against giddiness. It seemed to me that everything was swinging round in circles one way while we were circling in another. The watch was going clockwise, the radar search was going clockwise, the compass card was going clockwise — while the ship was swinging counter-clockwise, turning westward while the earth and all its instruments turned east. . . . We were out of phase — runaway —

You might say that as a result of my being unable to keep the last elusive vision of our fate from fading into utter blankness I abandoned all initiative, sacrificed myself, even my very consciousness, to O'Hara, who possessed my power to think and will to act as does a hypnotist. It was almost the mystical surrender of love.

"Passing zero-zero-zero."

"We got our chance to go to hell now!" proclaimed one of the awed lookouts.

Someone rang the wheelhouse, I could hear the standby helmsman mumbling into the phone. Then he shouted up the tube, "Wheelhouse to bridge —"

"Bridge —" O'Harra barked.

"Fantail lookout reports vessel astern on port quarter — so close he can see it in the rain."

"Desprit Christ —" exclaimed one of the lookouts.

47

"Shall I put on turns?" the standby helmsman yelled up the tube.

"Hold your speed," replied O'Hara moderately.

"Fantail lookout reports she's got lights! Shall I turn ours on?"

"Negative." O'Hara's voice, instead of growing fainter with the disapproval he normally showed for unsolicited suggestion, in the instant of crisis and peril rang almost endearingly with a firm paternal tolerance.

But the standby helmsman was on the edge of panic. "He says she's so close he can hit her with a heaving line!" His voice shrilled through the wheelhouse.

A brief pause and O'Hara said, "Tell him when she's close enough for him to piss on, let me know."

At three-five-zero O'Hara called for midships and at three-four-zero he met her with fifteen. "Steady on three-two-seven," he told the helmsman gently.

"Three-two-seven, sir."

"Range and bearing to the vessel ahead." His audacity was incredible. But also incredible was his fatherly tone. I realized in amazement that he was literally happy. He sounded like a man under morphine, lucidly at peace with the world and himself.

"Steady on three-two-seven," the helmsman sang.

And even more incredible was the radar data. I checked it twice to be sure, though I could not check the astonishment in my voice.

"Ship ahead bears three-two-seven — range one-oh-double-oh!" Whatever O'Hara's allowances had been he had put us precisely on!

"Very well," he said on the intercom. Though he was capable of the irony I read into the phrase, his reply was purely procedural. After a moment he added, "Notify the captain. Then sound the general alarm."

The accuracy of his calculations, the arrangement of his plans and spacing of his orders, even the rhythms that marked his replies were more than clockwork. They were poetry. His judgment and his timing had been flawless. And his nerves were superhuman. He should have been an officer on a man-o'-war; he was by instinct, gland, and brain a warrior. His almost aesthetic compulsion to impose his vision of order on men and nature, which was the appalling burden of his exceptional powers, in this instance had paid off. He was exonerated. It would have been impossible to do it better. It seemed impossible that it should have been done this well, and impossible, after I stopped and reset the watch, that on the trackless face of time there existed nothing more concrete than before to show that it had been done at all. But it had, and it existed as absolutely as the orbit of the oldest planet. Yet grateful and awed as I was over the phenomenon, I felt that I somehow in a strange and inexplicable way hated O'Hara for it.

One half-hour later the rain stopped at a stroke, as it had started. While we held intact our little enclave with the guide, two ships had been torpedoed, and their lurid pyres hellishly licked at the pall of night and the ghoulish silhouettes of the survivors. Three ships had sunk and nine were disabled in collision. Their hapless captains had failed to effect O'Hara's apocalyptic reconciliation of image and reality. Three destroyer escorts were dispatched to screen the stragglers. The convoy, scattered over sixty miles of ocean, was two days re-forming. It was, for such a maneuver, regarded as a remarkable record.

O'Hara's performance had been too extraordinary to be exemplary, but it had not been, as the Old Man's always was, and would have been I was sure had he carried this one off, a matter of heart. O'Hara's creed was not the tradition uncritically valued of being his brother's keeper. Nevertheless, I soon realized that he had made more than practical and technical judgments, that he had simultaneously made moral ones, had made them in combination with the others, which accounted for the profound quality of his achievement and distinguished it from sheer virtuosity. The Old Man would have been satisfied to have saved the ship. O'Hara's gratification reached far beyond that.

His only comment in our subsequent discussion of his exploit was to accuse us scornfully of the pious trust that whatever the predicament the Old Man would take care of it, would pull us somehow through. He was no believer in heroism, and there was something at once impressive and repellent in his will to organize the obdurate, recalcitrant facts of human existence without the heart to embrace its perilous sentiments. "You can't go around forever counting on somebody else," he said superciliously, "can you." It was not a question and so did not require an answer, fortunately. For his part, he was not content merely to recognize a truth. He had to prove it. And disturbingly enough he had.

"I still don't see how in hell he did it," the third told Costello in frank admiration. "How he could tell from a few early and lousy ranges and bearings that the ship ahead had lagged on her turn, and how to allow for it. It was all in his head."

"He gambled," said Costello, in whose opinion there was no science aboardship above the machinery spaces.

"The Old Man didn't seem to think so," Simms said. And Sayles, the complaining second, in whose view luck invariably meant adversity, was inclined to agree.

The Old Man had stopped by the open door of O'Hara's stateroom instead of calling O'Hara to his office.

"Mr. O'Hara," he had said in his deep patriarchal voice, "I commend you on a remarkable feat of seamanship." This was unprecedented, as by his silence O'Hara recognized. Commendations were not the Old Man's policy. In fact he believed that you raised men above themselves by assuming their fallibility and implying the constant need to prove their performance. "Mr. Sayles," he would say automatically after a casual glance around as he came on the bridge, "why are we off station?" And when Sayles denied being off he would say, "It looks so to me," thereby giving Sayles the dramatic satisfaction after a round of ranges and bearings of proving his virtue. As a result of this psychology the *Belle*, in spite of her lumbering awkwardness and inferior equipment, usually kept the best station in the convoy.

"However —" the Old Man had continued in a tone that justified O'Hara's wariness, "I must ask you to account for not notifying me in advance of the maneuver."

O'Hara must have expected this, for he was heard to reply quickly, "You had already been thirty hours without sleep. There wasn't much time and the thing was complicated —"

"Complication and sleeplessness are part of my duty, Mr. O'Hara. Concern for me is not appropriate to yours."

"I had it under control," O'Hara said shortly; exasperation had begun to drive off his wariness. Not that he wanted to be thanked; he merely wanted to be let alone.

"So it seems from the results," the Old Man retorted. "Nevertheless I am surprised, Mr. O'Hara. I understood you believed that a man's reliability was no substitute for the law's."

"I do," said O'Hara, "but the situation —"

"The situation," interrupted the Old Man, who was in fact honoring his mate by discussing principles with him, "I understand as one where the law was undependable, and the man might have been but fortunately was not. I say fortunately because it was not the law but him alone, with a little luck, standing between us and perdition. I am not reprimanding you. On the contrary, Mr. O'Hara. Law prescribes the action for most men, though not all, for most situations, though not all. This was one of the rare cases where the prescription would not have been effective. Cut it where you will, inside you always find a man. Lucky for you and the rest of us this time, you were the man. But I am talking about something more than you or me or any man. What I am doing is reminding you that it is the master's license as well as the mate's that is at stake —"

51

"I had that in mind!" O'Hara snapped.

The Old Man severely ignored the implication. "— And that occasions for breaking the rule are exceptional. And I am cautioning you against mistaking in the future these occasions for leaving the master's authority out of account."

With that the Old Man had stomped back to his office. But O'Hara, who might have been pleased at this unusual bending, took it morosely, as if on O'Hara's own legalistic terms the Old Man had maneuvered them both into an untenable position.

So each, feeling as he did the knifelike sincerity of his ways to a degree that more ordinary and evasive men did not, took unto himself his particular loneliness. Both accepted it and the painful conditions of it from choice and conviction. Yet even here was a difference. The Old Man was austere and felt his aloofness as part of the way of living he had elected, while O'Hara regarded his as part of the way he had elected to face living. Each in a sense, in his own way, was a puritan. Each was an egotist, but where the Old Man's ego asserted merely his own competence in his duty to a difficult and imperfect society, O'Hara's implied an invidious comparison with the incompetence of others in his unacknowledged urge to dispense with imperfection. Thus the traits they had most in common were what set them essentially at odds.

This contradiction seemed a snare to me, an example of the impossible combination of affinity and disaffection inherent in all human relations, and I resolved once again never to be caught in anything like it.

7

THE DRIZZLE had at least for the moment ceased. Drifts of flimsy clouds created a fluctuating memorial twilight in the wheelhouse haunted reminiscently by men now absorbed in another layer of time, including even the young meticulously indoctrinated naval officer who had been, about us and this hulk that had once been our world and life, so outrageously right for all the wrong reasons.

This vessel, aboard which our curious derangement had transpired, was as I have indicated one of the oldest of the Liberty ships, and by war's end one of the thinnest and flakiest. Yet she had been a veteran of some of the toughest going, and for a cheap, hastily built carrier she had been in her own way a somewhat dowdy heroine. Hers was not the career that fired the spirit of a man-o'-war, but in any event, in every event — some of them harrowing in her essential helplessness — she did her necessary unromantic job. That is to say, she did what she was constructed for longer than was expected of her. She delivered, and survived her expendability.

Her crew, like her, had been serviceable perhaps beyond their design and qualifications. If they came to feel her unworthy of them, it was only after she ceased to serve in the gallant if perfectly artificial trade of life and death. Until that time, both vessel and men, improvised into the intimate organization of ship and ship's company to a common end, had served that end unremittingly, faithfully, without presumption or encouragement.

Then one night she lost her bow in the midst of a Mediterranean storm. If casualty began at any one point, hers — and ours — might be said without our knowing the full nature of it to have begun here.

On that night, Captain Blake had shown the cut of his seamanship, standing in the wheelhouse, his great-boned trunk braced against the bulkhead, roaring for full rudder right and full rudder left as the *Belle* wallowed, shuddered, plunged, and her masthead light went under and she sank mountainously down and down until it seemed she had lost consciousness and the will to survive.

When almost before she had staggered to the surface at last, headless, the engine room rang the wheelhouse to say that they were taking green water down the stack, the Old Man bellowed, "Tell Mr. Costello that's the reason he has pumps!"

Below in the machinery spaces the black gang began pulling their off-balance bodies toward the ladder till the chief wound both legs and his left arm around a stanchion, took his automatic from the log desk drawer and turned it on them, yelling, "I'll shoot the first son of a whore that puts a foot on that ladder."

The second assistant engineer screamed at him, "She's going — we'll all drown like rats —"

"No!" Costello yelled. "We'll do it like men — in good order down to the last god-damned gasp! I'll tell you when to drown . . . !"

The second assistant looked sidewise through the fog in the direction of the sucking pumps, the booming shaft, the lights dimming and glowing, shook his head at the senselessness of this sanity, turned and waved the men back. Then Costello put the automatic away in the drawer, for he saw that it had been a momentary thing and they would all do what they could, at their stations, shut in like engineers, where they could not see it coming.

In the wheelhouse the second mate slipped on the deck, which was slimy from vapor caused by the seas avalanching against the portholes, and lay with a broken collarbone. The mate lashed himself to the port wing, the third to starboard, both screeching bearings into the wheelhouse when they could see the light. The Old Man sprawled on his belly on the deck long enough to work the chart, howling, "What's her head . . . ? Give her hard right . . . !" And the stand-by helmsman would shriek, "She's not taking it — she's not taking it!"

But eventually she did take it, kept taking it, though her stern mounted and her screw ran loose in midair shaking her like an earthquake as she buried herself forward, making the second howl from the deck where he lay, "The for'ard bulkhead won't hold, Skipper — won't never hold — cain't hold in this. . . ."

But what the Old Man bawled as he worked the chart was, "Hard right — what's her head . . ? hard left . . ! midships . . . meet her. . . !"

Bowless, she did not act like a floating object at all. She heaved, lurched, yawed, bogged, and stuck like an old sow struggling in soft mire. Though our feet were in the air half the time, we gave her the rudder, which she always suspensefully took, wondering how the Old Man had any idea what he was doing — like an expert horseman he simply felt her. The bulkhead illogically held.

All in a second, before the mates lashed to the open wings had seen the land in the darkness, she wrenched as though the earth had caromed off another planet, grounded herself, and the seas hit her astern like dynamite, and her lights went out.

55

We gazed down from the wheelhouse at daybreak straight into foaming water, as if the *Belle*, like a tormented ostrich, had buried her head deep in the earth. She was headless, half a ship, something such as you might see in an amusement park.

Two days later they got all of us safely off. Except for the forward third of her which was on the bottom of the Mediterranean eight miles out, the *Belle* lay virtually intact on a sloping shore. In Alexandria everyone marveled at the exploit of keeping a bowless freighter afloat for more than an hour and beaching her out in such a gale, that is, until they saw her captain, who in his great gaunt age looked as good as supernatural.

We bought the Old Man a gold wrist watch, engraved, which he refused to accept. He did not believe in rewards for achievements that were in the line of duty. "I never lost a ship," he said gruffly. "I had no mind to lose this one." We had it re-engraved and offered it to Costello, then to O'Hara, who were prevented from accepting it out of a kind of professional puritanism. So after a fourth engraving we gave it to Sayles as compensation for his broken collarbone.

He was touched to the point of fervor by this particular token of solidarity because he lived by his watch, not in a practical way since he was usually unpunctual and had no gift for planning his time, but reflexively through nervous tic. He did nothing without consulting it and consulted it without doing anything. He made persistent conversation of it. It was the last thing he looked at before going to sleep, when he wound it, and the first thing after opening his eyes, when he wound it. If he woke in the dark he switched on the light long enough to read it before dozing off again. It was not a means of ordering his life; it was an end in itself. He would continually compute the narrowing interval to meals and watches. And arrive late. He checked it when he rose from the table, when he met you in a passageway, at the top and bottom of ladders. On the bridge he would

56

clock the *Belle's* run between buoys and to O'Hara's contempt miscalculate her speed. Once a day he would compare his watch with the chronometers and fuss over how much it was gaining or losing. Its errors made him extremely insecure. To the annoyance of the ship's company, some of whom gained attrition by falsifying their responses, he would ask insistently, "Tell me, so-and-so, what time have yew all got?" He would be thrown into consternation so that he could hardly wait to rush for the chronometers whenever he differed by three or four minutes from watches he knew were inferior to his. "I don't understand — somethin' must be ailin'," he would say alarmed, shaking his ear clinically against his wrist.

At every opportunity to go ashore, instead of heading for the nearest bar like most of us he went in search of a jeweler, till finally he was informed that a predictable loss of fifty-six seconds weekly was as close to accuracy as this particular watch could be brought. Even that trifling mechanical instability nagged him so that he synchronized with the chronometers every Sunday at the instant of noon to reassure himself that his error remained constant. So he was overjoyed, not so much at having a better watch as at having two watches to compare with one another, until one day the bosun smashed his, and Sayles out of sympathy gave him his old one.

The Old Man got us survivors' pay, which, the officers told us, took all his influence. The *Belle* was floated and towed into drydock, where we went to see her more faithfully than if she had been an invalid mother laid up in the hospital, all save O'Hara, who failed to see the point of welding good steel to scrap iron.

8

IN THE MEANTIME we had a holiday. We rode out over the sand hills to shoot fat desert rats; we viewed all the tourist curiosities, relics of civilizations that had unaccountably gone to pieces in time. We probed the bowels of the city, the catacombs where were interred the bowelless bones of ancient potentates and their women, their sons and grandsons unto the third and fourth generations. On the highest spot in Alexandria we viewed the red polished shaft of granite known as Pompey's Pillar, which dominated long after Pompey the sultry allure of this Middle East, this sweaty midriff of the globe. But we kept regularly returning to visit the ship in her convalescence. She held us together.

They worked constantly on the *Belle* so as not to tie up the dock for too long, and most of us were as anxious as anyone to have her back in commission. After a while it became hot and troublesome living ashore. The wind blew mercilessly day in and day out, the southerly khamsin, blasting up off the Sahara, dry, dust-laden, and in excess of patience. We had nothing we had to do, there was no routine for us; we were bored and at loose ends. Gathering on the dock morning after morning to check the *Belle's* progress, we began to see her growing bow as representing a curious, far-reaching kind of wholeness. Otherwise we were scattered and without aim.

Then, in one unguarded moment, the war simply ended. It seemed to us hardly possible that so massive an action, so long in the making and extensive in the carrying on, could have ceased, without any world-shaking and decisive climax, upon the midnight. The tremendous momentum of a tremendous concerted effort had simply ground to a standstill, leaving millions of tons of equipment, thousands of ships, including the old *Belle* in drydock, scattered over the earth surging against the sudden stop.

The war had ended as though it had concluded nothing, therefore signified nothing, and, because it seemed at the moment to promise nothing, as though its ending merely prolonged the lives of those who had survived it. The crew lost their sense of common cause and condition, unable to see themselves as participants in the deeper general destiny secreted in nature.

Our achievement in the fundamentally incomprehensible turmoil of the world now seemed an illusion which peace had reduced to a shambles. Some of us went out on a round of the bistros to celebrate an event we hadn't felt or witnessed, feeling that we had been stealthily cut adrift from coherence.

So we began to celebrate this, and coming out the door of one café as we were going in we met seven bluejackets, who were also celebrating the unreality. One of them bumped into our bosun and swore arrogantly at him.

"Sorry," Bohunicky said without enthusiasm.

The bluejacket turned to his mates. "How's about that?" he asked rhetorically. "He says he's sorry." He turned back. "You sure you ain't yellow, buddy?" he asked Bohunicky. Bohunicky nodded. "So," the bluejacket said, "you are yellow."

"Naw," said Bohunicky. "I said yeah, I ain't yellow."

59

"How'd you like to prove it, buddy?" inquired the blue-jacket.

Bohunicky, sullenly figuring the odds against us, shrugged fatalistically.

"Okay, buddy," the bluejacket said. "Let's go around back with our buddies here, boys."

We all walked around the corner between two buildings and fought like Goths. This was something Bohunicky and his two friends, a French Canadian and a Georgia cracker named Parsons, took naturally to. Their idea of the best possible liberty was to go ashore, get likkered up, and then fight each other to exhaustion, after which they would return aboard torn, bruised, bloody, grinning, happy and sheepish with their arms around each other.

But there was no sport or joy this time. When it was over seven bluejackets were lying in the dark alley, and we went looking for some other part of town with our hands in our pockets. "Sons of bitches asked for it," said Bohunicky. We naturally agreed, but from then on we drank without celebrating.

From then on also the group that checked on the *Belle* grew smaller each day. She had ceased to be home and mother and had become that lousy old Liberty. One morning I found myself on the dock alone. Several of our men, I knew, were in jail. None of us had seen the steward in two weeks. The Old Man was reported to be ill, and one of our engineers named McKay we heard had been picked up in an alley in Arabtown stabbed to death in the neck.

Meanwhile the khamsin blew.

On the dock I noticed Costello. It was the first I had seen of him since the ship's company had been quartered ashore. He had a woman with him, so I kept my distance. He left her and came over to me. "*Belle's* being undocked Saturday," he said, rolling his head around to wipe his thick neck under his silk shirt collar with a silk handkerchief. He looked soft and temperamental with all that cheap silk. "The Old Man ain't doing so good," he said. "You seen the Mate?" I told him I had not, and asked him if he wanted me to try to locate him. But he had already left me and I did not go after him because of the woman.

After the *Liberty Belle* was finally alongside, the crew came up the gangway in driblets of two and three. Even the steward appeared, though how he learned she was afloat no one knew or cared to ask him. She lay tied up at the pier, starboard side to. From stem nearly to superstructure she was brand-new and freshly painted, while the rest of her remained used up and covered with streaks and scabs of rust. This gave her a split personality weird to see. But her bright bow pointed seaward, and unconsciously in our minds its original significance had altered to a vague promise of home. The war over, she would be going back. That was mainly what brought the men around for a few minutes each day to see if the expected sailing orders had come. That too was the basis of their feeling of dislocation when the *Belle* moved her berth and simply tied up to another pier.

She changed berths for no apparent reason three more times during the next month, while the khamsin kept on blowing. Our eyes and skin were stung by this abrasive wind, our sweat was gritty, and the airborne dust penetrated our shoes, making raw the skin between our toes. The very atmosphere we breathed was flying sand.

The rumor began to pass around that the Old Man was not fit for sea. At first this was hard to believe, he was such a crag of a man. But little by little what was sheer speculation became accepted, in the weeks of shifting and grumbling, as indubitable fact.

Bohunicky, who used to swear that Blake was the best goddamned master in the United States merchant marine, growled, "The Old Man's over the hill. Why don't somebody get us a skipper?"

"O'Hara?" asked a seaman dubiously. "Ain't he got papers?"

"Son of a bitch —" said the bosun, who knew as well as any of us that O'Hara was qualified.

"Nobody gives a goddamn whether we got a skipper," the seaman said morosely. "Nobody gives a goddamn what we do — go to sea, go home, go to hell, or rot in these stinking parts. I tell you, Boats — nobody even knows we're here. The old *Belle's* liable as not to lie around till she pits through and sinks at her moorin's. They've forgot about us."

9

THIS WAS our growing conviction — that the great invisible organization which joined and directed us in enterprise had simply lost track of us, or had cast us off to be shunted about making way for those who still belonged, eventually to drift out of sight out of mind in chartless seas. Each man, in disgust, jealousy, and resentment, went his separate way, wherever that led him, and no one worked aboard the *Belle* to speak of.

Then one day word got around that we were taking on cargo. Unaccountably the crew returned aboard, except the Captain, the engineer who had been stabbed, and the two seamen who, after being released from jail, had disappeared and were not heard of again — all as if some mysterious toll was slowly being taken.

Loading and stowing cargo was the responsibility of Chief Mate O'Hara, whose frustrations were not improved by the fact that he was punishing himself ashore, drinking. He left much of the work for the other two mates. The second, when he was operating under the surveillance of someone else, was fairly adequate and content. Like many men of meager capacities he relied on conscientiousness to get him by, made a fetish, made a virtue of it in self-defense to compensate for inherent lack of ability, and was righteously indignant at officers with executive capability who practiced what O'Hara was fond of calling "dynamic indolence." Because he saw a job only in terms of its details it looked larger and more impossible to him than it was, and he had to be everywhere at once, with the result that he unconsciously dreaded responsibility, not being able to assimilate it. It taxed him to the extent that he had long ago developed a single deepening scowl of worry that slanted across his forehead like the line of a fraction.

Though he wheedled and cajoled them, he got far less work out of the men than either of the other mates, and far more breakdowns. He had always treated the crew fraternally, as if as second mate he was merely the instrument of their equivalent humanity, actually as common a man as any other in the undistinguishing, reductive sameness of human brotherhood. He was their friend, their partner. By preference he often ate with them and drank with them, and invariably he thought and felt with them. He preached their common duty instead of exercising his own. Since he regarded this as the only right and decent relationship among men, he eradicated the distinction of position and function through a kind of comradeship in obligation, insisting he was no higher or better or different than anyone was. He even stood between the crew and orthodox discipline, to the annoyance and concern of O'Hara, and defended them against its arbitrariness as being an affront to their dignity and sensibility.

All this had worked passably enough under the common risks and pressures of war, and the men had usually spoken fondly of him as "a regular Joe," and felt free to unload their views and grievances on his indulgent ear. This gratified him inordinately and encouraged him to preach the wisdom of his policy as far as O'Hara's unsympathetic, skeptical ear. But now something had gone sour. The men, including the bosun, became critical of their ally, took advantage of him, argued with him, complained about him — his blundering and in-decisiveness — on all sides and to his face. He could not comprehend this betrayal of mutual interests, and grew harassed. And the more he was harassed the harder he preached his gospel, and the worse their attitude seemed to get.

So he stewed and preached and sweated, and resented O'Hara's going ashore at midafternoon each day, leaving him in charge, and returning aboard late the next morning red-eyed, pale, and relentless. He sputtered continuously to Simms, who was openly amused by the state he was in — after all it wasn't Simms's neck.

Invariably Sayles would waylay O'Hara, punctual even in his absenteeism, just as he crossed the gangway, and deliver a long plaintive rehearsal both of the problems he had already solved, or which had solved themselves, and those he clearly felt were utterly insoluble by any man alive.

He would by habit rub the deep furrow slanting across his forehead with one hand and keep repeating, "Ah simply don't understand — ah cain't understand it," as if the whole world were somehow just faintly and unfathomably in error. It was not that he sought help or consolation of O'Hara, he merely took comfort in apprising him of everything that went wrong as a subtle kind of disciplinary measure. Being a small man with a small man's long memory for impositions, real or fancied, he was punishing O'Hara, who was disdainful of all obstacles. O'Hara would glare impatiently at the second throughout his minute recital and, viciously imitating his Southern accent, would at length say with an exaggerated drawl, "Mistah Sayles, mah nose bleeds fo' yew-all! It is jes tew complicated." Then he would go drink coffee in the officers' mess for half an hour.

After he had gone the second would tenderly wipe the sand particles from the corners of his eyes and mutter his exasperation to the chief engineer, who had taken to doing his drinking aboard during the day. "Cotton!" Sayles would exclaim. "Egyptian cotton! Why are we takin' on cotton? Ah cain't understand it —"

"You should have my job," Costello would say moodily, pink blotches glowing on his cheeks. "Every day I steam it out below — one hundred and eighteen! Every night I have bad dreams!" spreading his hands. "I am not an engineer. I am a junk man."

Dockside was for Costello a lapse in function, an interval during which all time was virtually suspended, or replaced ashore by the cyclical life of the senses. Underway he lived like a master horologist, making his calibrations in terms of pressures in his boilers and oil lines, soundings in his feedwater and fuel tanks, and the revolutions hammered out by the tyrannical shaft in whose blind and thundering rotations all the measurements of his intelligence culminated. Like every first-rate engineer Costello entertained the opinion that he and his men made the ship, were the heart, lungs, and guts of her, and all those above deck were parasites living off his engine and sucking the blood of his gang. They should complain!

The crew quarreled among themselves, one accusing the other of not hauling his weight; some malingered feigning sunstroke; most argued with the mates when O'Hara was not around; no one stayed aboard if it was possible, as it frequently was, to sneak ashore.

Finally the maddening khamsin blew itself out.

On a Monday afternoon to everyone's astonishment, with only one hold three-quarters full, we were ordered to cease loading. The winches were stopped, the booms lowered and secured, cargo nets rolled up and stowed, hatches dogged down. Thousands of bales of cotton remained piled on the dock.

The second accosted O'Hara as he was leaving the ship. "What kind of game is this heah?" he asked, rubbing his slanted frown. "Ah don't understand —"

66

"Ah sho nuff don' know, Mistah Sayles," O'Hara rasped. And he went on his way.

Chief Costello, watching him depart, observed, "Don't blame the mate. He's done what he could."

"How's that?" asked Sayles suspiciously.

"Well," the chief said, chewing a burnt-out cigar, "The Old Man's got a galloping case of atherosclerosis and a touch of senile dementia among other things." He had obviously relished mastering this technical jargon. "O'Hara's been tryin' to get himself skipper an' the feather-merchants on the beach won't pay no attention to it. The Old Man refuses to disqualify himself, and he's got the pull to make it stick, it seems. Won't give up — can't get used to the idea he's just passin' through."

Sayles, dumbfounded by the medical terminology and the politics of command, said querulously, "I knew it was bad luck our gettin' mixed up with this heah lousy cotton. Don't nobody care what happens to us?"

"You johnny rebs never quit bitchin' about your luck since you lost the Civil War, do you?" Costello observed disgustedly. He spat his cigar butt overboard. "Why should anybody care? They got their own troubles."

That was on a Monday. Four days later on Friday the Old Man at last came aboard with sailing orders.

"To Salonika!" the second wailed to Costello. "In the name of . . . with half a hold of cotton, why Salonika?" And he set off to round up what could be found of the crew.

"Why anywhere?" replied Costello somberly, staring over the side.

The Old Man had gone at once to his cabin and rung for O'Hara. He looked ghastly, gray of face and dead of eye. His flesh had shrunk from his great bones, he staggered slightly on his monumental legs, and his blue hand fumbled on the latch when he opened his door. He kept to his quarters for the following three days while O'Hara bitterly got the *Belle* ready for sea.

In retrospect I could see how all these elements were fitting together, unbeknown to us at the time, to form the pattern of our destiny. The Old Man, who at the outbreak of war had pulled every ruse he could to get back in service, regarded his command of a wretched Liberty ship not even as a sort of extended longevity, but as if he were embarking on a whole new career, a second lifetime. Unlike O'Hara, he was committed to the character of command rather than the style of it. He would have accepted with dignity the command of a garbage scow or a raft if it had fallen to him. It was the fault of his moral tenacity which had been, which was, his virtue that he could not conceive of there being any morality in bowing out of responsibility, or vice in clinging to it. In addition, I suppose, like other men he simply did not wish to grow old and die. Had he not been the prodigious figure he was, with the reputation he had had and deserved, he might have experienced difficulty earlier with his chief mate.

I could see what ailed O'Hara from several of the things he was incapable of concealing any longer. The system, the organization, was ruthlessly grinding him down. He had begun to detest everything and everybody because he was fit to be master, and knew it. He had the load now, without the authority, and this galled him the more. The Old Man lay in his cabin above him, cheating him of that without being able to utilize it himself. The Old Man, for all his personal ability and achievements, had also had the luck O'Hara did not believe in. O'Hara had come to view himself as the victim of fools and dotards, a fall guy. And what was more galling still, he hated himself for having been maneuvered into negatively coveting the command of a ship they cared nothing for. They would not even give him what, for a man of his qualifications, was not worth having. The incapacity and indifference, the failure in judgment on top of him worked on his nerves, his self-esteem, his sense of order and justice. He simply could not function as master without being master. What had made him an admirable mate under an admirable skipper would have made him an admirable skipper, but under a failing skipper made him a failing mate.

Early on a Tuesday morning the tugs sprung us out and we got underway. The Old Man came on the bridge, nodded to the pilot, and sagged into his chair, where he sat without a word, staring out ahead. He looked ninety. There was none of the elation and ritual that normally pervades a ship which casts off from prolonged dockside hurly-burly, clears the harbor, drops the pilot, mans the watch, takes departure, lays her course, and settles down to her business on the high seas.

In the channel the *Belle* passed a British destroyer, but no one took it on himself to dip our colors. The destroyer dipped hers anyway. When it came time to drop the pilot the Old Man let him leave the bridge with a mere nod and no escort. Presently he lumbered below himself.

The cruise, begun badly enough, got no better.

We rode anchor off Salonika a week, unexpected and unwanted. After that we steamed to Bengasi, then to Tripoli, then to Messina. After that to Naples. Even with her brand new bow nobody seemed inclined to trust a cargo to the *Belle*.

We went apathetically ashore, past vessels being loaded at dockside, and envied their crews cursing the work. In the bars we got known as the liberty boys; weary merchant seamen referred to the *Belle* as "the liberty yacht," and on their side envied us our idleness and freedom, finding beyond comprehension our chagrin at having no assignment.

Once in a bar in my hearing the normally convivial Costello ventured the theory that the Old Man was not anxious to press for a cargo for fear of making himself conspicuous to somebody who might get the idea he should be retired again, for good and all.

"Have you gone asiatic?" a fellow engineer incredulously inquired. "Play it up, man, play it up."

"I'm asiatic, I guess," Costello told him. "I must be."

"It's no skin off yours," the engineer advised. "Get drunk and get a woman. See the world."

"I have," replied Costello. "I could enjoy that more if I wasn't so damned free to."

The engineer finally gave him a long penetrating glance. "Have a beer," he recommended, nodding in confirmation. "You're asiatic."

For some time Costello had in fact frankly complained of a certain symptom of malaise. He had observed in himself a loss of libido which he now confessed to his colleague because it hit him where he lived. It was not merely that he took a liberal joy in fornication, he viewed his potency as the significant index of his health and vitality, and its decline caused him to fear that he was deteriorating. He did not want women so much as he was made nervous by not wanting them more, and the fact that he had consulted two doctors, both of whom had humorously if not admiringly dismissed his alarm, increased his contempt for the medical profession and did not in the least reduce his anxiety. As a result of this he had become a hypochondriac and was beginning to show a moroseness unnatural to him.

For myself, I held apart and bided my time. This was not my portion, not the one I was seeking, not anything resembling what it must and would be. It was a passing dumb show, having nothing to do with me. My purpose, if not specifically defined or directed, remained at least aloof and pure.

At each port it was fantastically the same; we neither loaded nor unloaded cargo. The Old Man stayed in his cabin most of the time without discernible improvement, while O'Hara appeared to be running the ship. At any rate, punchy as we were getting to be, his ill-temper was the single obvious force that kept us functioning. It was our scourge as well as his.

At Naples we received orders to proceed to Port Said.

". . . I wouldn't believe it was possible if it wasn't happening to me," Simms, the third, exclaimed. "By God, we've been two months cruising all over the damned Mediterranean with a hold full of fluggin, and nobody knows what to do with us. We're orphans, by God," he said to O'Hara. "We could do anything we wanted to. We could turn around and head for home and nobody would know the difference or care if they did."

"Why home?" O'Hara had sourly asked. "As well go anywhere. Have no illusions, Simms. Nobody *does* give a God damn!"

With the seven seas to cruise over we had, it seemed, no port of call, no point of reference, so that instead of the joy in illimitable freedom you might have expected, we felt we were drowning in it. We experienced simply an increasing premonition of looseness and entropy.

Three days out of Naples I woke about midnight to that soundless void which comes over a ship whose engines have stopped. For a second, before it came to me that we were not in convoy and the war was over, my heart also stopped. Then I settled back with no more than the general apprehensiveness instinctive to sailors. But being unable to go to sleep I decided to get up and find out what the trouble was. On my way I passed one of the black gang going off watch who told me they had let the lube oil pressure get low, with the result that one of the bearings had been badly scored. This was unheard of from Costello's men, and so it struck me as a major calamity.

When I came to the door by the engine-room ladder I saw the Old Man bending against it, bracing himself against the bulkhead, his profile lit spectrally by the light pouring up from below. The chief engineer's antagonized tones rose from the hush and hiss of the machinery spaces.

"Keep a cool stool!" it shouted. "We got no place we have to get to. So we goofed off — what's so goddamned serious about that aboard this ship?"

"Mr. Costello —" the Old Man roared in something like

his old voice, and immediately he gulped for breath. I could see that he was trembling all up and down his long arms and legs, and his huge head was shaking as if with palsy, while the veins and tendons beat and twitched in his emaciated neck. "Mr. Costello — turn all hands to on repairs around the clock. I do not propose to wallow out here like a cripple or a derelict. Whatever this ship is she is our responsibility." His entire torso swelled with his next breath. "If we never have a place to get to, you will keep your organization down there!" he thundered. "We will hold our course aboard this vessel if the whole world goes to hell . . . !"

He painfully straightened himself, looked at and past me unseeing, like a sleepwalker, and started back to his cabin, one hand trailing weakly along the bulkhead and his slippers whispering over the deck.

10

AT PORT SAID three days later we anchored out. There was no more to go aboard than in previous ports. We took on fresh stores under the supervision of the steward. The Old Man remained in his stateroom as if he had suffered a relapse following his ultimatum to Costello. From habit only we thought about leaving the ship.

To go ashore from our mooring it was necessary to employ the services of a water taxi, which the steward soon enough procured for the ship. He had a special gift for procuring anything that was wanted, always at bargain prices, from jewelry to foul-mouthed parrots. "That's too much," he would habitually say in his purring tones of a prospective purchase. "Let me get it, it won't cost you half." And it never did. Or, wearing his sagacious smile, he would produce for you some article you had scoured the area for without avail. He had a sixth sense for seeking out and taking an advantage.

He made a shrewd business of trafficking in the various appetites, and it was in a business way only that most of us had anything to do with him, or he with us. He apparently, so far as we could tell, received no mail, had no possessions beyond the bare necessities, no friends, no family, and wherever he went he went alone. His name was Ermitt or Armitt, few of us knew exactly because he was generally called Armpit even to his face.

He was the sort who no matter how clean he might be always looked unwashed. Yet he kept himself, you might say, obscenely immaculate. Several times a day you would catch him slipping with his secretive smile into or out of the shower, although he never appeared to sweat. His flesh was molasses smooth and without blemish. In the worst climates in spite of his rapid and constant movements his skin never glistened and his shirt never revealed the dark spreading stains of other men's. His metabolism was perfectly attuned to and at home in the most hot and fetid atmospheres.

He had a pockmarked complexion the consistency of coke, muddy brown eyes, thick bright lips which he licked continually with a snake-like flicker of the tongue, and a knack of making you think he was winking slyly at you without ever fluttering an eyelid. There was about him the air of a being who, having once gazed into the pit, has not looked away again, who would do anything, not for himself but for you. I imagined him, while restraining himself, treacherously encouraging and abetting others in the most unspeakable licentiousness. For all the women and liquor he provided for the crew, he was never himself detected in the use of either. It was impossible to tell what he did with the money he pocketed.

He had not been known to overstep, or make a clear-cut mistake. His discipline of himself, his manner, was careful, too careful, as if he must be indefatigably on his guard, forever anticipating everyone for no ascertainable reason. It made you uneasy, intimidated you, convinced you that at any time he chose he could ambush you with his uncanny foreknowledge of something you had gone around blissfully and stupidly unconscious of. After a thorough but fruitless search for some missing article he would quietly discover it in the likeliest place, which to your bafflement you had overlooked.

74

You felt your vulnerability in the face of his obsequious self-possession. He carried himself with discreet assurance. He had the alert reticence of a man who knows human susceptibility, and he catered to this susceptibility with a virginal lover's peculiar combination of abjectness and power. Even in his most craven, pandering gesture the confidence of depravity shone darkly within him. He was fascinatingly repulsive, an indescribable contradiction, but he produced. We could not put in at a port where he had not been before. He was on terms of obscure familiarity with them all. At Port Said he produced for us the dependable services of a water taxi while other vessels took their chances or went without.

In his subtle, evasive fashion he had from the outset been a dominant if intangible influence on the entire ship's company, up to and including O'Hara and the Old Man. He served their austere comforts scrupulously. There was always hot black coffee on the bridge and never a dirty cup lying around when you were through with it. The officers' beds were made up within a half hour of being vacated. It was extraordinary the way he got around. You felt his presence everywhere, yet nowhere in particular. No one knew where he slept, if he slept; at no hour of day or night was he to be found in his bunk. He seemed immediately on call, and since you knew you could summon him in a twinkling — almost without calling, almost with the mere inward impulse, the unvoiced and even unrecognized need — he seemed there with you when he was around the corner and around the corner when he was there.

Simms tolerated him, Sayles got on with him charitably, the engineers made the most use of him except for Costello, who, in addition to living for slightly more gourmet pleasures than the steward provided, somehow suspected him of being connected with the stabbing of McKay in Alexandria. The Old Man treated him as though he were a well-oiled machine, but O'Hara detested him on some nameless instinct. Whenever he was in sight O'Hara held an unwavering, baleful, and frustrated eye on him as if his presence itself was to be distrusted, and in his absence constantly conducted minute inspections of his operations in the saloon and galley for an opportunity he did not get to catch him out of order. It was as though O'Hara found obnoxious the very perfection of those services which Armitt sensed exactly how to adjust to the temperament of every other individual aboard so that the rest of us came unwittingly at the cost of our privacy to purchase without valuing them.

Visitors from other ships marveled how adroitly and assiduously he spoiled us all. "Nobody," they averred, "ever had it so good at home." In this way, through the hardly noticed details of our often rough shipboard existence, by easing, he eased into our intimate lives, and suavely and unobtrusively enslaved us to his unspeakable stewardship.

A connoiseur and expert of the lusts and vices in which he appeared never to indulge himself, a minister to others' pleasures and weaknesses, whose only pleasure and weakness, duty and devotion, was in that, he also had some skill in alleviating the ills resulting from these pleasures and weaknesses. Except in cases of serious injury or disease, where the Old Man administered first-aid, he generally acted in the capacity of ship's doctor. This was in keeping with his function, this clearing away the debris of the appetites so that they might not stale or sicken at sight of their refuse.

It is well known that during oppressive periods of waiting, on protracted cruises, in ports where there was no liberty, vessels with doctors aboard were swept by a fad of circumcision. Medically this was justified as physical and mental hygiene. Armitt, not qualified to provide this diverting therapy on the *Belle*, provided instead a satisfactory professional substitute through the art of tattooing. By war's end there was not an epidermis aboard save mine, the mate's, and the Old Man's, that did not exhibit prominently some of his virtuosity. On Costello's right arm he had etched a woman, a hard cliché of hearty pouting lustiness shockingly epicene on Costello's stout male flesh. Down the muscles of Bohunicky's hairy upper arms he had created a chorus of nude females who undulated distortedly with the flexing of the biceps. Simms had settled for a pair of fouled anchors on the inside of each forearm, but Sayles had the most elaborate of all, the masterpiece — a pastiche on his scapulae of Mary Magdalene washing the feet of Christ, from a picture in one of his books.

The steward himself was clean of such adornment. In ascetically plain but startling letters he bore with arrogant fatalism on the muddy skin over his heart only the macabre, dire, knowledgeably evil legend:

BORN

TO

DIE

It affected me as the most striking and revolting of all. I could not think of him, stripped to the waist or with his shirt on, without seeing every capital letter in vivid gangrenous black of that infamous tattoo.

As a matter of fact, from the moment we anchored at Port Said I did not see him again till nearly the end with his chest covered. Bared all this time, that execrable, nauseous formula flashed everywhere about the ship so that it seemed to be needled into your very sight.

It was in full view during an incident that occurred our first afternoon in port. The steward had arranged to have the Arab from a bumboat, hanging cautiously under our stern, vend his trinkets on the after deck. He had exercised his usual cunning about the place, and about getting authorization from Sayles, who was easily persuaded against ship's policy that the transaction would accomplish two humane ends by simultaneously raising the morale of the crew and the standard of living of the filthy wailing Arabs, for whose degradation Sayles doubtless felt his habitual sympathy.

Half the crew gathered on the fantail to bargain listlessly

for the shabby wares which the Arab, slinking aboard, spread out on mats. The steward acted as interpreter. His ignorance of Arabic was no barrier since he could communicate with any devious intelligence regardless of language. Sayles stood by in an attitude of benign and slightly foolish brotherliness. No one was really interested in the Arab's goods. The main point of the affair was diversion, the sort you get by carelessly browsing around a carnival.

With the Arab were two skinny women and half a dozen rickety urchins of both sexes, all of whom silently obeyed his crackling authority with quick and furtive moves.

"How's about that?" one of the black gang observed to another. "Your kids and old woman jump for you like that?"

"Like that!" replied the other snapping his fingers.

"You lie," said the first. "They won't none of 'em. That's what ails the country. Women an' kids ride all over us. Look at that filthy old bastard, will you! He's got it made. Like a rotten admiral. Got two of 'em an' six kids, an' probably more home. Why, my old woman would act so mean I'd have to go out an' get boiled."

"Trouble with you you ain't the man he is," said the other.

"Bet?"

"Ten."

"You're on."

"Armpit —" the first one said — "ask him how much for the women."

Sayles took a step forward. "Quit that," he said chivalrously. "It ain't proper."

"Who's proper?"

"They're his wives," explained Sayles morally.

"He's a scurvy bigamist," argued the engineer.

"That's proper for him," Sayles said.

"He can keep 'em," said the engineer. "They're pigs." Sayles smiled indulgently.

"How much for that?" a deck ape inquired of the Arab, pointing to a camera.

78

The Arab motioned to one of the women, who snatched up the camera and held it up but not out. The Arab extended his insinuating hands, fingers spread.

"Dollars?" cried the deck ape raucously. "You lousy thief! It's an American camera. You stole it an' now you're tryin' to rob me for it." He drew back his arm threateningly. But the Arab stood in his squalid pride and did not flinch. "I ought to take it away from you, you lousy thief."

"Quit it —" Sayles again intervened in a brotherly tone.

"But he's stole it!" the deck ape protested puritanically.

"Wal," Sayles said in a conciliatory drawl, "suppose he did. It's still more his than yores."

"Why so?" argued the deck ape. "I'm an American ain't I? All's he is is a stinkin' thievin' Ayrab!"

"He's got his rights," said Sayles.

"He got a license to steal?"

"He needs it more than yew, it's his bread an' butter."

The deck ape was enjoying himself. "He don't need bread an' butter. He eats dung." There was general laughter. "Besides," he added in a plaintive tone, "I need it. I need it to take some snaps of the *Belle* to send home to my poor old mother." The laughter was louder.

The Arab's body jerked energetically as he jabbered away with his incomprehensible sales talk, and his eyes glowed black and shrewd.

"Ask him if the women ain't for sale has he got any feelthy pictures," put in another sailor.

In the burst of laughter the steward pointed to the camera and made a gesture in the international language of obscenity. The Arab at once showed his jagged yellow teeth and squawked at one of the small boys who obediently started forward.

It was at this point that things broke loose. O'Hara, who had been lying in his bunk presumably asleep, had happened to step onto the boat deck and seen what was going on. He went back inside, got hold of the third engineer, and ordered

79

him to cut in full load on the fire main. Then he sent the bosun Bohunicky with two men to man the after starboard firehose on the boat deck, and walked out to witness the result.

When Bohunicky opened the nozzle on the two-inch hose the stream of salt water under about a hundred pounds' pressure thundered like a cataract onto and across the after deck below, cutting the legs from under those who were standing in its path. Its deadly white shaft sought out the mats and drove them smashing in a cascade of worthless articles against the bulwarks. It then sought out the hapless urchins, strewing them scrambling about the deck frantically trying to get their feet under them long enough to reach the rail. They succeeded and jumped overboard, end over end at first, then like cats recovering themselves in the last twisting instant and landing succinctly in the water. One by one the stream sought out the women, who turned away clutching the rail, with their heads down, as the water hammering their backs gave off a hollow sound as of drumming on a gourd. Finally it sought out the Arab vender, who faced into it in a position of supplication, smacked him full in the belly knocking the breath out of him, and in the face blinding and drenching him with a hard thudding spray as he crouched openmouthed, till he looked like an aquatic statue in a park. The whole spectacle had the aspect of some cruel baptismal rite.

Sayles, recovering from astonishment, raced to the bulkhead underneath where Bohunicky and his men held the hose and O'Hara stood staring down. The last of the gamins scrambled over the side, but the women remained huddled back to at the rail. The crew after scattering to the sides yelled with glee. The steward had disappeared.

"Cut it —" Sayles's voice mounted in a wail to the boat deck. "Turn off the hose!"

Bohunicky glanced at O'Hara, who stared down steadily and without expression. After one of his significantly timed pauses, without looking at Bohunicky he nodded. Bohunicky pulled the handle on the nozzle and the decks fell silent. The bedraggled Arab squatted as if in a pile of half-washed laundry while the water streamed off him.

"That ain't human —" Sayles whined at O'Hara, sobbing with breathlessness.

O'Hara at last contemplated him directly. "Who's human?" he said. "The rule is those rats are to be kept clear of the ship."

"Let 'em go," Sayles whined angrily.

"Secure the hose," O'Hara curtly directed the grinning Bohunicky.

"How'd yew like to be used that way?" Sayles said accusingly.

O'Hara gazed incredulously down at him. "Not likely I'll have to worry."

"They got a right to be used like humans," Sayles persisted.

"I don't get you nigger-lovin' rebs," O'Hara snapped. "You should know by now that junk is all stolen, most of it from American ships. They'd steal you blind and dumb, if you weren't already. For a quarter in the dark they'd slit your throat."

"They got to live, like anybody else."

"Why?" O'Hara said simply.

"It's this treatment makes 'em steal from yew. Use 'em right so they can live an' they won't go thievin' off yew."

As Sayles turned away the Arab, who had remained transfixed in the ecstatic posture of baptism suddenly leaped up, scuttled across the deck, and flung himself on his knees at Sayles's feet. Seizing Sayles's left wrist in both his black claws, he struck his forehead against it several times scattering drops of water into the air. To everyone's amazement he began to repeat shrilly, "We go — we go — we go. Sahib thanks — sahib thanks!"

In embarrassment Sayles withdrew his arm and said, "Yew go home. All right. Yew go home." He waved toward the

81

heap of rubble that had been sluiced against the after bulwark. "Take stuff. All right. Go home."

The Arab, his gandourah hanging in soggy folds, backed away salaaming and intoning, "Sahib thanks — we go — sahib thanks. . . ." He yapped briefly at the two women still huddled over the rail, and they scampered ahead of him toward the stern.

We watched them go through the pathetic motions of gathering their flooded articles into the mats. When the women went over the side carrying the mats like sacks, the Arab salaamed his way back across the deck, dropped again to his knees, as in a religious ceremony, and pressed into the right hand of the dumbfounded Sayles the camera he had priced at ten dollars. As before he clasped Sayles's left wrist, struck his forehead several times against it murmuring, "Sahib thanks —" Then he salaamed his way to the side and in a second vanished over it.

Upon his usual slow recovery Sayles strode rapidly astern, leaned out brandishing the camera as the bumboat rowed rapidly off, and shouted, "Come back! Yew keep! Sahib got! Yew need. Come back!"

But the Arab, as though he could not hear a word, faced stolidly forward and proudly and graciously allowed himself to be propelled away by two of his boys till they were lost amid the other bumboats milling about the harbor.

Sayles solemnly paced across to O'Hara, who contemplated him from above with a curious glint in his eyes that seemed to illuminate and suffuse his whole countenance.

Holding the camera aloft in triumph, his voice breaking inarticulately, Sayles said, "Yew see heah — yew see. . . ."

O'Hara's inflamed blue eyes gleamed down upon him a long moment. "I see," he said at last. "Tell me, sahib, what time have you got?"

Then he turned deliberately and walked to his room, leaving the rest of us foolishly gawking at the band of white skin on Sayles's upraised left wrist.

11

TWO DAYS later Armitt, incorrigible steward of our lapses, was reported to have recovered Sayles's watch, though this would not have come out if Costello had not pressed from him a slippery half-admission. But how he had repossessed it no one could corner him into confessing.

Sayles in the meantime had been in a state of agitation over the loss. It had discredited his faith and corroborated O'Hara's cynicism, and it had sent him into a sentimental funk because the watch was the one the crew had given him in Alexandria. But above all it was the best watch he had ever owned, and by dint of constant calibrations the most accurate one aboard. He regarded it as irreplaceable. To a fraction of a second it had given security to his days, and on the innumerable instances during the forty-eight hours of its absence when he inadvertently glanced at his wrist he was shocked to confront only a pale sinister band of incalculable flesh.

Therefore, discovering it when he woke in the morning, where it lay quite mysteriously obvious in the center of his desk, he was overjoyed nearly to weeping, and after winding it and setting it by the chronometers was at once able to conclude that the Arab had repented and returned it surreptitiously at great risk, sneaking aboard like a thief in the night, thus reaffirming the virtue inherent in delinquency. With this persuasion he at first stoutly rejected Costello's testimony to the contrary. And to tell the truth, since the steward had not been observed to leave the ship there were others as well who doubted his reluctant insinuation.

But when it was implied that the steward might be lying where he could hardly be caught in it, to gain credit he did not deserve, and his reluctance was explained as a crafty ruse to gather additional plaudits for self-deprecation, he became one of the maligned delinquents in the mind of the second, who shifted his sympathies from the Arab to him and took up the defense of his modesty and fidelity.

When O'Hara got wind of this confused affair he scented a connection between the steward and the bumboat and set out to fix him with responsibility for conniving at the Arab's coming aboard. But everyone from the second down, though they knew better, denied his complicity here. The boat had simply come alongside and the second had allowed its occupants to come on deck.

"Why push it?" Sayles protested. "The watch is back."

"The watch is back," O'Hara echoed, caustic and mocking. "That's not what's important. You can always buy a watch. What's important is you don't know why or how it got back."

"It's a mystery." Sayles passed it off shrugging, resigned and content.

"A mystery is dangerous," O'Hara said.

"It's past," Sayles argued, "and theah's been no harm."

"A mystery is never past until it's solved," O'Hara told him darkly. "It goes on. It reproduces its kind."

The steward himself found it expedient under O'Hara's relentless probing to deny knowing anything except by heresay about the restitution of the watch. It was as much a mystery to him as to anyone. He had accepted credulously from the start the second's explanation, and only let pass

84

the ambiguous hint of his authorship under Costello's assault in order to save the anchor watch from being hauled on the carpet for letting the Arab creep undetected about the ship under their noses. No, he had seen the Arab neither before nor since his slushing down.

O'Hara, who could not function unless his lines were clear, was inadequate to this sort of tangle. "You're a lying toad!" he said to the steward. "One of these days you're going to make a slip, and I'll be waiting for you." To Sayles he observed in his moment of unguarded exasperation, "The Old Man won't always be standing in the way."

At this point Sayles's passionate outburst astonished everyone. "Yew cain't wait to take over, can yew — so's yew can pain us all." He shook his finger in O'Hara's face. "Yew want to make us suffer. Yew ain't human. Yew got no care for us an' our feelin's. Ain't a man ever knew yew didn't hate yore ugly guts! Yew know what a sadist is? Wal yore a sadist. Yew'd like to git yore hands on this ship so's yew could twist an' torture us. Yo're just waitin' an' hopin' for the Ol' Man to die!"

Here he suddenly ceased his tirade. Everybody stood silent, a little thrilled to hear O'Hara spoken to like this.

Defiantly Sayles said, "Go on — go ahead an' try it!"

"Try what?" asked O'Hara stiffly. It was obvious he had been put off his balance.

"Whatever yo're thinkin' of." Sayles fumbled and wilted, he was gone all at once.

O'Hara looked around. "I am trying to think of you as men," he said slowly. "I am having a devil of a time." He drew a great quick breath, almost as if Sayles had got to him, and turned away.

He could be generous enough, and even kind, where that made any sense to him. I did not doubt he felt the pain of others, and regretted it, but he took it as a measure of existence and was incapable of believing that every man should not like himself expect and be expected to bear it. His view was abstract, like his passion. Sayles mistook this for in-humanity.

From exasperation O'Hara sank into bitter apathy, but he rallied enough spiteful vigilance so that Sayles was obliged to report to the skipper's sickroom for a guttural, half-coherent reprimand from the exhausted old man for reviling his mate and permitting the venders to board his ship. Sayles took this gladly, vaingloriously even, for it made him out a hero once more.

The relations between steward and crew were so complex and confused that while they might use him, scorn him, mis-trust him, fear him, be damaged by him, they could not give him away. They protected him as you would a confidant or accomplice you despised. He was as damnably safe from dis-closure with them as he would have been in the confessional, and they with him. They would risk their own involvement to hide his, and he his to hide theirs. Sometimes you wondered if it was not the most perverted subreption of loyalties.

For taking the brunt as he had, they united in favor of Sayles, and for the first time since the war had ended ceased to badger and defy him.

The ironic upshot of the whole episode was that this be-came Sayles's sole consolation, since the watch, inexplicably affected in the adventure, thereafter refused to keep anything but the wildest sort of time, now losing three minutes of a morning, then gaining six of an afternoon. But it had be-come a symbol of a new kind of order and comfort, so Sayles wore it anyhow, as though he felt less exposed with it on, and at intervals he could be found contemplating its aberra-tions with a mellow, uncritical gaze.

About the middle of the first week in Port Said I con-sented to go ashore in the evening with Simms, persuading myself that nothing could be worse than the intense heat of an iron ship without mechanical ventilation. We rigged wind sails at every possible opening, but there was no wind, and the *Belle* was like an incubator. I had never known up to that time such a fermenting atmosphere. The air always seemed to taste insidiously of rich rotted fruit of some exotic kind; overripe and cloying it hung on you humidly, clung to you, coated your tongue, swam in your sight, crept into your ears and under your armpits like fungus.

Simms and I were about the same age, and though he came from a lower-middle-class, Middlewestern background and had only a middling education, I supposed if I or he had anything in common with anyone aboard it would be with each other. He was sociable and intelligent, and had advised me while I passed the time studying for my third mate's license the year before. He had an instinct for learning and using all the angles and was generous and unapologetically frank about pointing them out. He had been of great help to me generally despite his unventuresome attitude. He had a kind of opportunism without daring which I did not like, not so much because it was serious as because it admitted of nothing more serious than itself. What could be had readily and without strain he took; he was totally deficient in a sense of high adventure.

When I came out on deck it was an hour or more until the long subtropical twilight would begin. Simms was already standing by the accommodation ladder, talking to the steward. They seemed to break off at my approach.

"Let's go," Simms said, with what struck me as uncomfortable and pointless importunity.

The water taxi was waiting below. I caught in the steward's lover-like, concisely roaming eyes that look of intimacy which, though he never forced you to, you could not directly meet, and as I descended the ladder after Simms I took full in my vision on its clay-like flesh the nihilism of that black, menacing tattoo. I boarded the taxi and we set off across the harbor in the direction of town.

"What is it about that steward —" I said, swallowing as though I had a disagreeable taste in my mouth.

Simms was regarding ruefully the growing darkness down the front of his clean khaki shirt.

"What about the steward?" he asked preoccupied.

"Born to die —" I quoted disconnectedly and in distaste. "What does that mean?"

Simms got out his handkerchief and mopped his face and neck. He was obviously not particularly interested in discussing the matter. "What it says. What else?" He dismissed the subject with a tone of subdued indifference, and I did not choose to press it. During the trip we hardly conversed at all. It was too hot even for speech.

We no sooner disembarked from the taxi than I regretted lacking the strength of will to take it back to the ship. Going into this town suddenly became an unhealthy, a contaminating project. I hung back disheartened. Simms wanted to see, as he put it languidly, whatever there might be to see. But I suspected from the way he set out that he had some prospect in mind.

"Come on," he said negatively, "you can't tell what will come your way. Right? The idea is to get what you can out of what's available — even in a dump like this. What else have we got? The *Belle?* The Beautiful Liberty? You want to go back and rot in the rotten Liberty?"

In the oven-like calm of the late afternoon I tagged after him at a squeamish pace, lagging along, for all my attempts at underexertion perspiring through my shirt. After the first hundred yards all I wanted was a shower. "I suppose the town might be a little better," I said, consoling myself with the recollection that anyway three minutes out of a shower and you were as soiled as before. There was no escape.

"Couldn't be worse," he cheered me neutrally. "At least it's different."

I remember thinking then how I had all I could do to cope with the familiar — it was what was different I was afraid of.

"Doesn't it ever rain here?" I said, irritated.

88

"It rains," replied Simms. "And when it does the whole world steams like a Turkish bath."

Not far from the waterfront we encountered a knot of merchant seamen milling and shouting and scuffing sand. In the circle I recognized Bohunicky and several of our men.

"Somebody hurt?" Simms wondered, veering aside toward the melee. "Probably heat stroke. They been ashore all day."

But as we approached we heard a strange primitive sound of snarling, and between the legs of the men caught glimpses of two little mangy yellow curs fighting murderously. One of them breaking loose tried to run, but the men closed in with their legs so that he fled in circles seeking an outlet, the other dog darting after him. The fleeing dog in desperation charged the barrier of human shins and was kicked back into the center of the ring, torn and bloody. There the other fell frenziedly on him and the senseless carnage continued while the men urged and cheered.

The losing dog tried again to make a break for it, got half-way between the legs of Bohunicky, who, dense and immovable as a heap of slag, squeezed him off from escape till he thrashed in the sand in his terror and screamed. The other dog was on him once more, tearing at his haunch, when amid the snarls and the flash of fangs too swift to see Bohunicky staggered, and the mangled dog instantly raced away for his life, a chunk of raw bright flesh and yellow hair flapping from his hindquarter, lethally pursued by the other.

With hardly a change in the sound of shouting the circle shifted so as to surround now one of its own. Bohunicky stooped in the center grasping his left calf with both hands.

"Son of a bitch —" someone yelled, "you let 'em go!"

Bohunicky straightened his square body. "Son of a bitch bit me!" he yelled back.

"Our dog won. You pay us."

The Bohunk shook his head and shouted, "No contest — no contest! Your dog bit me!"

While the tumult rose the accuser was pushed violently

into the center against Bohunicky, who swung on him re-flexively. The other struck back and that was all it took.

"Finish it off!" the onlookers yelled in furious jubilation. "Winning side takes the money!" So they closed in opportunistically, whooping up the fortuitous solution, and the two men began to slug out the gamble in the dusty heat and sand.

Simms took several steps in the direction of what had been a dogfight, ascertained that Frenchy and Wentworth were on hand, and came back where I was standing. For a moment he seemed about to make a comment, changed his mind again and simply shook his head a few times, slowly. I had no wish to prompt him. I had been thrown off myself on feeling my heart pound and my own hackles rise.

Bohunicky, ordinarily humorous and peaceable, once started fought without care, without skill, with brute strength and manic abandon. I remembered the alley in Alexandria, his silent head like a cannonball, his short deadly arms and thudding fists like connecting rods, his squat impregnable body, and afterward his eyes as expressionless as the pale steel of ball-bearings when he startlingly confided: "Someday I think I'm going to kill somebody. I think about that all the time." He had smacked the bleeding knuckles of one clenched fist into the palm of his other hand. "I think someday I'm gonna flip."

When he had rolled sideways toward me his bulbous eyes, agate-hard and so protuberant they were hardly protected by the sockets they started from, I thought for a fact that they must bulge from an excess of pressure inside his skull. And when in alarm I had advised him to get help, see the Old Man or a doctor, or both, he had grunted. He was dangerous, as he knew himself, because it was almost impossible for an ordinary man to hurt him, even with a club, or hurt him enough.

I also recollected the wild agility with which he had fought the boom gone adrift from its lashings, swinging from its topping lift, leaping on it and riding it with the eerie sham-

90

bling grace of a gorilla. Excitement, any excitement produced in him an insanity of purpose capable of equally frightening feats of good or ill. Frightened and mystified by this potential himself, with a kind of aboriginal helplessness and innocence he had taken the only civilized recourse he knew and sworn his two biggest shipmates, Parsons and Frenchy, who were also his friends, to pull him off anyone he was beating if they had to knock him unconscious. He never went anywhere without them if he could help it.

From beside me I saw Simms make a depressed gesture. "Let's stand clear of that," he said, moving toward the town.

To conserve effort we willingly economized on conversation. I felt a disadvantage going into town not sharing what lethargic initiative Simms had, having at the same time no desire to share it. He kept glancing up and down the littered streets caked with mud, along the dun walls baking in the sunless evening heat, as if hunting for old landmarks, though he claimed that like me he had not been in Port Said before. I had the sensation of being completely out of bounds, as if I were doing something felonious for which I might be picked up and remanded to some authority any minute, and after a while with great misgiving realized we were wandering on the outskirts of Arabtown. At length Simms wound up at a place with a sign which read LA CIGALE.

"La Cigale — we are here," he announced. "What's it say?"

"It's French —"

"Yeah — yeah," he said, "I know that. What is it? La what?"

"I'm not sure," I said. "I think it's grasshopper."

"Go to the grasshopper, thou sluggard — consider her ways and be wise. Why not?" he inquired with false enthusiasm. "I'm thirsty as hell."

12

THE PLACE we entered was as windowless as a dungeon and as dimly lit. By the time we took a table and had our drinks the lights were out altogether and a dancer vaulted from nowhere into a spot of garish light in the middle of the floor. Virtually naked she writhed and insinuated herself toward the pale greenish faces that turned like the underside of leaves in response to a gust of wind. Slowly she arched backward till one hand touched the floor beneath her head and her clavicle, ribs, and pelvis — the frame of her animality — articulated themselves through her heavily powdered flesh with appalling candor as, with her free hand, she threw a spangled streamer onto one of the tables, did a handspring and landed on her feet. She snatched up her streamer and repeated the maneuver several times, each time in a different direction while the faces turned and turned.

"Would you look at that!" exclaimed Simms. I looked instead at Simms. There was a glistening intentness in his gaze, and at each toss of the streamer he jounced slightly in his chair. To a tantrum of sound from the band the dancer whirled past the tables in a series of cartwheels and flipped out of sight behind the shadows, leaving the stale sweet odor of overheated, perfumed flesh on the faintly agitated air.

Before the applause had quite subsided a little girl scampered out dressed like the dancer. Her skinny arms and legs had a sallow sheen under the light. Preoccupied with the routine of her movements, like a perfectly trained dog, she flaunted her bulbous childish belly to the rhythm of the band. The applause, whistles, and catcalls were delirious. She might have been eight years old.

Following her dance the lights came on. Simms occupied himself by ogling some of the more palatable women at various tables. It was a while before I could get him into conversation, but when I did he grew quite happily confidential.

I had asked him, "You enjoy this sort of thing?"

"I enjoy life well enough. I could never see the point in not," he observed sagely. No, he wasn't ambitious. He had been an ordinary seaman, but he hadn't gone to the maritime academy from ambition. "I keep my finger on my number and let the next joker do the same, that's all. The way I figure it, being a deck ape I had the whole system on my back. You can't enjoy much that way. You have to get out from under some of it. You can't beat it, so you better play along, join it enough so you have some of it under you working for you. But," he cautioned, "not too much under you or it also gets too big — too much of a load. I mean, it wouldn't be worth it. The great thing is to get what you can, do what you have to, play it cozy. Above all, never sweat it."

He wasn't preening himself on his wisdom, he wasn't being smug. This was simply how he sized up the heavy problems of living, and given his premises, and somehow or other his aims and values, his solution appeared honest, intelligent, and correct. I too, I told him, found pleasure in being alive, but for me it was bound up with the possibility, the threat, the inevitable risk of its opposite — of pain. I thought pain was important as an index of something more serious than merely making out.

I said, "If everyone viewed it like you, we would have all

mates and no skippers, and the mates wouldn't have jobs because without skippers we couldn't put to sea."

"Check," he agreed, leering at me tolerantly. "But not everybody does."

"Suppose they did," I theorized.

He gaped artificially at me. "What sense is there in supposing that?" he inquired. "Everybody won't."

"You count on that?" I asked lamely, knowing that his statistical fact had made my moral hypothesis look silly.

He gave me no quarter. "On what else?"

My drink, some kind of cloudy citric concoction of Egyptian gin, was sour, and between sips I had to work my tongue and cheeks so that the saliva would wash the taste out of my mouth. "And you think they're suckers — the ones that sweat it?"

"In a way," he said, deftly balancing his interest between the talk and the other tables. "After all, we're only passing through, as Costello says."

I had him in profile, a good even profile, and he was throwing his words my way from the corner of his lips. He was a good even man altogether, bronzed and frank, and normally he met your gaze straight on. He was aware of you even when he was aware of other things. But he had no distinction because there was nothing, absolutely nothing excessive about him. He was unmarked. This explained the curious fact that he had no nickname. He was called simply Mr. Simms, Simms, or the third. He was never in difficulty and he never suffered the minor accidents and injuries usual aboardship. He did not lose his temper or drink too much. Pleasant and smooth, he got along with anyone, in any circumstances, because his measurements were infinitely adjustable.

Just as I was marveling at his perfect equanimity he faced me all at once with the faintest wavering shadow in his eyes. "Look at O'Hara —" The sardonic note had momentarily gone from his voice. "He's eating himself alive. What good is it doing him or anybody? Less than any good because his

94

kind cause themselves and everybody trouble. And if it did any good, what would it amount to ten, five, a year, one month from now? Things just go on and on." He waved one clean large bronze hand conspicuously around the dark room to indicate an unending series of circles. Could it be, I suddenly caught myself wondering, that the source of all his attitude was fear? "He's kidding himself!" he said fiercely. "Why if the poor bastard dropped dead tonight the world would move right into his little space as though he had never been there. In fact it's already crowding him and he isn't dead yet." Then, almost wistfully, as an afterthought he added, "It's crowding all of us."

I thought to myself that it certainly did seem to be, and said, "Don't you believe in holding it off?"

"Sure," he said, "only I don't believe in success the way O'Hara does. I like O'Hara, for some reason, but I wouldn't be him. A man like that has got to get more of the breaks than most of us."

"What does he want?" I inquired, thinking I had an answer. "He doesn't seem to care whether you like him or not."

"Maybe," Simms said. "Maybe he don't care if you hate him either. He wants whatever gets him respect — not approval, everybody's respect but mainly his own. The son of a bitch wants what can't be measured and can hardly be enjoyed. He wants the damnedest thing of all."

To a waiter Simms held up his empty glass in one hand and two fingers of the other as though he were making the victory sign.

"Not for me," I told him, sucking at my cheeks to make the saliva flow.

He shrugged. "Might as well let him bring 'em and if you don't change your mind I'll drink it. It *is* pretty foul." He had reverted to his earlier position and mood.

"How can you work for them if you don't put any value on their view?" I asked him.

He widened his eyes in mock schoolmasterly fashion.

"You're mixed, son. I don't work for them really, it only looks so. That's where they kid themselves. They work for me. By taking a job I wouldn't have they make mine possible. Slick, hey?" He narrowed his sidewise gaze. "You think I don't value them for that?"

I gave it up. What threw me off my stride was his believable if atrocious honesty — the honesty of an extremely rational animal. But so far as men went there was a contradiction. He was putting a premium on the middle, whereas by definition a premium was what was put on the first, the leading. He was putting the middle first. It was all out of whack.

When I told him this he widened his eyes again. "You're still mixed, son. I'm leaving it right where it is — where I want it. I'm not putting any premiums on anything. All I'm saying is that's the place I — me — Simms, third officer of the *Liberty Belle*, prefers to be. I leave all the premiums to you and O'Hara."

"But," I still protested, "look where you are now — where we all are."

"All right," he said, screwing up his face. "So I make the best of it I can. This society I've worked for my own use has used me as cynically, and by my complicity I am to blame for my own predicament."

"Well," I said with some respect, "no one can accuse you of not having the guts of your lack of convictions."

He shrugged again, resplendently. "Not guts," he said. "It's just the way it goes. And where does any of it, any of us, come to? That's what O'Hara's never asked himself. Yet." He made the motion and sound of spitting into the air. "Born to die. You read it now?"

This time I did give up, since it was becoming a matter of words. Was Simms potentially, except for his attitude, a first-rater? Over my half-finished drink I brooded on it while he drank away at my second one. He nor I nor anyone would probably ever know because he would never take the critical test. He protected himself with adequacy against the risks of excellence.

96

13

DROPPING the discussion as soon as I did Simms had
gone over to his original preoccupation, examining the
women, meeting their eyes, smiling at them with significant
geniality.

Whether it was a response to one of Simms's glances or
an inductive response to his glancing in general I did not
know, but she came slowly and thoughtfully out of one of
the dark recesses of the room and sat down between us, a
woman not young or old, dainty in a slightly scraggly and
careless way, with a continuous stare. She smiled and did
not smile.

She was, I was aware though I seldom noticed women's
getup in any of its ridiculous detail, fairly well dressed and
completely self-assured. There was a wart on the back of her
delicate left hand nearest me and a mole in the left corner
of her mouth. Her really thin, rather demure lips were made
imperfectly to look bold and opulent by extending them
with lipstick in a bright cupid's bow upon the skin around
them. Her shadowed eyelids gave a reptilian quality to her
wide shiny eyes, her hair was swart and glossy, but her perfume was conservative and more oblique than what I could
smell all around me. Her breasts were noticeable without

being large, and there was the usual lipstick on her front upper teeth. You had at first the sense of contradiction between her somewhat tawdry surface and what you thought you saw beneath.

Leaning breastily against Simms she said, speaking good American English, "I like blond men with fair skin. So I came over."

"Welcome, welcome," Simms replied ironically, and I thought strangely with a touch of discomfort. "Only the brave deserve the fair. Have a drink."

Laying a dainty hand on his leg she said, "I'm hungry."

"What'll you have?" Simms asked magnificently.

Stretching from her waist she pulled aside his open shirt collar and buried her face in the hollow of his neck, while he sat there wearing an expression of fatuous astonishment. "Mmmmm—" She purred like a cat, settling back and contemplating him with cat-like intensity. "I'll have more of that."

Still he sat, a smear of lipstick on the skin of his neck, looking as if he had just been bitten by a vampire. Finally he recovered and said, "Who are you, doll?"

"Well," she replied slowly, "I was a tourist once. I suppose you'd call me a whore now. I laid over in this place too long." She gave a thin shrill little laugh. "My husband was an American businessman, so I'm a whore. It wasn't his fault. But I'm a poor whore. I'm too zany. I eat up men, especially blond ones with fair skin. I love them. If I didn't have to live I'd only do it for love, if I could do it often enough." Her voice trailed away. "When you can't get enough there's really nothing else, is there honey?" she explained, with a sad vestal resignation.

She glanced sidelong at me so that I felt myself shrink. Simms had a frozen smirk on his face. There was something fearsome in the bald, incongruous frankness of her lechery, which now communicated itself not merely through what she said but in every aspect of her — the shiny well-like dusk of her eyes, the instinctive caressing movement of her slim

98

brown hands upon the air and in the direction always of Simms, the yearning posture of her slight torso, the way her skirt slid up her separated thighs not by intention but as an unconscious expression of personality, almost of style.

She seemed, this slip of a woman, to reduce the whole of life to unabashed bodiliness, the abandoned aggression of which made Simms apparently as well as me feel, especially after the masculinity of our earlier conversation, like children whose world has disintegrated before the onslaught of an overwhelmingly mature fact. It rendered her slender form absolutely gigantic.

Here was the fundamental wisdom, the overpowering honesty. I sighed with relief for the moment like a man who has discovered the philosopher's stone. All cares, all concerns were annihilated in the concentrated sense. This was simplicity, security, this was the sanction of selflessness itself. It was so engulfing, so hypnotic in the candor of its irreducible terms that I was temporarily helpless.

I surmised that Simms was similarly so from the twisted, mortified grin he wore while she commenced gently to stroke the inside of his thigh. "Come on, honey," she wheedled. "I could do it often enough with you, couldn't I?"

"Zany is right —" he said, his voice cracking like an adolescent's.

If I had not been at least partially persuaded myself I would have had to laugh outright at Simms's excruciating ambivalence. He glanced at me apologetically and emitted a nervous snicker.

"Be damned —" he sputtered. "You lie in your sack all day and all night, month after month, and dream about having it thrown at you like this, and be damned if when it happens to you this way it don't put you off."

"What difference does it make what way it comes to you so long as it comes?" The woman looked at him inquiringly with her swarming eyes. "What's the matter, honey?" she said with a note of combined softness and strain. "Aren't you a big boy?" I could not help observing her increase the sweep of her caressing hand.

"Big enough," Simms retorted roughly, half in anger, so that I noted the change in his attitude. The current passing through and from him to her and back was visible.

"I thought so," she breathed comfortingly and comfortably. "I knew you were when I saw you all the way over here." She stopped her caressing motion and took him by the wrist. "Come with me," she murmured, softly guttural. "You know what I am, honey? I'm a Turk. I'll bet you've never been screwed by a Turk."

I thought Simms looked at me then with dumbfounded appeal, as if asking me to help him out. But I must confess I was in too deep myself at that point. I had somehow identified myself with him without at the same time actually having to be him, so that every staggering move she made toward him, every devouring glance she bent and intimidating word she breathed on him was happening also to me. We were both in complete thrall to some naked combination of allure and repugnancy. It was like drowning, where all your desire is to cease struggling, to sink, and all your fear is of the finality of doing so.

"I got my friend here —" Simms began, and finally when I gave him no assistance he added wavering, "If you knew someone —"

She turned her glittering tormented eyes on me. "I'm sorry, honey," she told me tenderly. "I don't travel that way. I'm a loner. Maybe both of you —"

The second she put her left hand on my leg it was like breaking a spell. My reaction was swift and convulsive; I felt my heart stop and my face burn, and I pushed back from the table and stood up, trying not to be too obviously hasty. "I think I'll call it a day," I told Simms.

He stared at me vaguely, his mouth a little wrenched, as though he did not quite comprehend what was going on. "Now don't hurry —" he said hesitantly.

I know now that he was making a final plea. Just a light hand, a trifle to start him out of it, was all he needed and all he unconsciously asked. A mere suggestion that he come along with me back to the ship would have done it. But I wanted to escape to myself, to be alone, and so I did not think to proffer it.

"There's no hurry —" he protested; still I failed to notice how he was torn.

"Yes there is honey," the woman said urgently to him. She took his hand she had been holding and drew it slowly along her own thigh underneath her dress, gazing darkly into his eyes. "I'm in a hurry, honey. Can't you tell —" Her voice dwindled beseechingly. "Can't you tell —" Became a flat, neutral, lonely, obscure whisper. "— I'm in a hurry —"

My gorge rose chokingly and the bill I meant to drop on the table for my drinks fell on the floor beside her. I stooped blindly to recover it, and when I straightened after seeing the flash of her full parted thighs under the table the blood was pounding in my temples, I was lightheaded, and I trembled as with a chill.

In my last view of them she had leaned back in her chair, her breasts heaving slow and deep, her eyes glazed and sightless, oblivious to everything else as if, spinsterish and ascetic, she waited only to be immolated by the ancient sacrificial knife. Simms, with his free hand tossing down the remainder of his drink at a gulp, was waving his glass in a reckless arc at a waiter and saying hoarsely to her, "Okay — don't rush me, Turk — I need a couple more drinks. . . ."

I fled the town and lost my way to the harbor, thinking on that fragile meat in its cruel ecstacy of slaughter. And somehow I felt as disturbed as if I had been in Simms's place, and something else Simms would not feel — an unpleasant suspension as though I had cheated myself, knowing all the while, as Simms no doubt knew too, the male disadvantage in the deed.

14

THE DENSE subtropical night had blossomed moonlessly by the time I got back to the ship. I mounted the ladder on the starboard side, drifted aft to the fantail for a minute, saw my taxi disappear among the running lights crossing and recrossing the harbor. Beyond them in the polluting haze the lights of Port Said glowed lurid and cheap, like sequins.

I had been trying to identify the preoccupied, haunted and haunting expression, a sort of retinal darkness, which I had seen in the eyes of the Turkish woman and Simms. I had seen it before, and I placed it now. It welled almost constantly in Sayles's eyes. I had observed it after he shot down the plane off Anzio, while he lay on the wheelhouse deck with his collarbone broken crying out that the bulkhead would give way, whenever a vital job he was assigned to became difficult or exhausting, or his watch stopped, or his sights failed to cut in to a usable fix. The same intensely dark yet glittering expression must have been visible if anyone had been on hand when he hovered over the hatches of tankers in the old days. It was in the eyes of others, Sparks for example, shredding his nails between his teeth over an abstruse problem in electronics, my mother during one of her attacks, the Arabs swept by the fire hose, the little yellow cur as he sought his frantic way out of the ring of human ankles. Recognizing it at last I wondered if it had been seen reflecting from my own eyes. I could not imagine it in the eyes of the Old Man or O'Hara. It was the look not of lust for life, but terror of it.

In the midst of these profoundly disturbing reflections I had heard the gently dipped oars of a native boat drawing aft, hugging the portside shadow of the ship so close I could not make it out. It passed deep under the ship's stern and softly out of earshot in the night.

Musing on the phenomenon of one of these bumboats so far out at such an hour, I went into the galley for something to eat. At the door I collided with the steward, who for a moment appeared actually disconcerted as though, in the way I analyzed it later, I had disrupted some errand on which he had been too intent. He recovered his obsequious poise instantly.

"Was that you in the taxi?" he inquired with his oily cordiality.

There was that about the question which struck me as being inconsistent with the circumstances of our encounter in some manner I could not quite define then. I was always ready to suspect him of being up to something unsavory and nefarious.

"Back already?" He made his noxiously overpolite, knowing smirk. His teeth were broken and his dogteeth abnormally long and fang-like. I nodded and shrugged. I wanted only to be rid of him, to have him go about his business whatever it might have been.

"Why go ashore?" he asked with his cunning emphasis, and that expression as if he had winked. Perhaps, I was not sure, this time he actually did wink.

While I gazed at him not altogether comprehending yet, he moved suggestively by me and I caught the flick of his moist muddy eyes before he vanished down the passageway. I smelled perfume on him as he went, a faint, cloying, sickly scent. Perfume! Even on him it astounded me.

What little appetite I had had at that hour in that heat was by then spoiled. I selected some sort of native fruit, thinking it would be chill-fleshed, crisp, and flat to taste, and took it out on deck. But it turned out to be as warm and pulpy as the air around me, so I tossed it over the rail and did not hear it strike the water.

Within two days I saw the steward come aboard with the Turkish woman. They came up the accommodation ladder in broad daylight. The woman had the appearance of a stark, elaborate doll. She carried a red and yellow parasol and her red and yellow dress fluttered invitingly at the hem in the burning air. In the tiptoe movement of her feet she hardly seemed to touch the scorching iron of the deck, yet I had the peculiar impression that if she were to brush ever so lightly against the rust streaked bulkheads they would be demolished. She had the appearance of a toy — a dangerous, hot toy like a firecracker. Something within me sprang like a cat in the dark, and I turned away just as the steward was escorting her out of sight into the living spaces.

It was on the fourth or fifth day afterward, as I remembered it, that I made up mind to shift my berth to the lifeboat. Apart from everything else, living topside was more comfortable and infinitely cleaner. My duties were all above deck, so that it was convenient to transfer the mattress off my bunk and the few things I needed out of my locker into the lifeboat. I chose most carefully one of the after boats because its location was more open as well as more airy. The tarpaulin warded off both sunlight and moisture, making me very snug and private underneath.

The water taxi from Port Said seldom came any more to ferry the crew, and though most of them were staying aboard none cared where I established myself, or bothered me where I was if they knew. I took anchor bearings periodically from the bridge and kept the log. I was entirely unconcerned with what went on below.

O'Hara had made one more try ashore to do something about the state all of us were in. It obviously failed like the others since he had returned aboard drunk, in that ominous way of his that did not show except in his more than usually bloodshot eyes, flushed face, and vile temper. He was almost eaten away by this time with a cancerous rage against the incredible stupidity of the system he served, which could be moved neither by reason or force to take steps no man would deny were clearly necessary for the welfare of everyone, including its own. A renegade Catholic who had exchanged one impervious system for another, he had been unable to work his way legalistically through either. You had even then the feeling there would not be a third. This was it.

O'Hara had come to feel so isolated in his own common sense and sanity that you got the idea his giving up, when it came, would not be an act of capitulation or conversion, but could only be one of anarchy. The theory of Simms was coming to pass in fact. If the system had filled the place with someone else, O'Hara could have taken that in mere frustration. What he was actually fighting was the danger of its annihilating him by getting along as if the place the Old Man had almost ceased to occupy, the place he O'Hara could and should occupy, was not merely unimportant but was not really there — as if the place any individual could and had to occupy existed nowhere except as a fantasy in his own cruelly hallucinated mind.

The night before we were to get under way for Freemantle I woke in my lifeboat and lay curled in a sort of fetal doze sensing that I had heard something. A few seconds later I recognized the stealthy plop and creak of a boat being rowed very close to the ship, down the portside as before, where there was no ladder. The noise was so faint that I lost it almost at once. My first thought was that I should perhaps take some action, if only to mention it to one of the mates, but I seemed to be in the grip of a strange inertia which deprived me of the instinct of initiative. It was easy to assume that the phenomenon meant nothing, or if it did that it was no affair of mine, and at daybreak when I roused again I had other things to think about.

By now it seemed to follow with entire naturalness that we should receive orders to proceed to Australia without augmenting or reducing our old partial cargo of Egyptian cotton by a single pound. The logic of what was happening to us was thoroughly understandable, even forgivable, so long as its pattern was the one you thought and acted in. No doubt as in the case of many another veteran of many a war, the peaceful world was having difficulty accommodating or assimilating us. Our continuity had broken off. Nobody anywhere having anything for us to do, we had simply become a paper entity, a troublesome clerical ghost, haunting shipping offices hither and yon, to be conjured with, to be exorcised and laid.

The absurdity of a nearly empty carrier being routed around the world for no other reason than as a bookkeeping device to clear the shipping rosters was, when viewed in this light, no longer absurd. It became, as helping fight a war had once been, our function, our destiny, and best carried out, you might well think, for purposes of the sibylline books we would never see, by our never showing up anywhere again to be a nuisance to anyone.

Whatever the reasons, or lack of them, for our being thus doomed, the fact was we were headed down under.

We were slow getting under way because the engineers had been late lighting off. When O'Hara had gone after Costello he found out, if he did not already know, how lordly a chief engineer can be. Costello, hungover, categorically refused to exert his authority. The challenge that had once kept him setting records with his inefficient plant he would no longer take up.

"She'd have been put to the torch long ago the way she

ought to of been if it hadn't been for me. I've kept the stinkin' bitch hot all this time," he shouted through his cabin door at O'Hara with his magnificent resonances hoarsened. "I'm through sweating just so you apes can sail the ocean blue in your yacht. It's an insult to a decent engineer. If and when my boys want to give you steam that's their business. What in Jesus' name does the Old Man think he's doing? Does he know? If he won't call a halt to this — well I can. I'm goin' to let her burn herself out. Without me you see how long it takes. I apologize," he declared fervently, "for not doing it before."

Whether O'Hara thought he could not handle the chief engineer, who as a matter of fact outranked him, or whether he did not care, I couldn't say. At any rate, all he had said was, "Have it your way," and returned to the wheelhouse. He had his own idea of who was the indispensable man aboard.

Our pilot was Egyptian, one of the first, and because the Old Man trusted only the European pilots he tried to get to his bridge. But he was too ill and had to be taken back to his cabin. The sight of him, gray and haggard, struggling with his weakness in the interests of a ship that had ceased to matter except to him, for an image of command that had no further correspondence with reality, was monumentally incongruous. His face was contorted with frustration when we helped him to his bunk, where we left him breathing in vast spasms through his teeth.

None of the crew showed on the weather decks in the arrogant sun as we entered below the fertile delta into the orifice to the grand duct of world commerce. Only the stand-by helmsman and I occupied the wheelhouse, along with the Egyptian pilot and O'Hara.

The pilot was tense and kept peering about as though he thought something was amiss. He naturally expected more officers on deck. "Captain sick?" he asked O'Hara, not lifting his glance from the marks. "Left five."

"Left five," O'Hara barked, giving the pilot an affirmative answer by merely closing for an instant his bloodshot eyes.

We furrowed past the opening lips and thrust our towering way into the canal, the low land stretched thin and membranous before us and on every side. One after another all the ships ahead and all behind penetrated this torrid isthmus, past egg-shaped luteous dunes, through the long vestibule to the Bitter Lakes, lying like a flattened pear, and, after about twenty hours, the narrow cervix opening on the Gulf of Suez.

Yawning with fatigue our second pilot left us at Port Sudan. He disembarked hastily with the cordiality of a man glad to get away from company that has made him anxious for reasons he would rather not learn. His intelligent eyes took us in like conspirators, without resting on us, and he seemed to avoid getting close to us or breathing deeply for fear we might be infectious. "I hope your captain is well before long," he said, showing handsome teeth, startlingly white against his black mustache. He spoke little, observed and thought much. He was an impressively dependable man.

O'Hara at the rail nodded sourly and proceeded to the charthouse where he laid our course through all the ancient myths of the Red Sea, whose waters are held to have once parted to let pass a dispossessed people on their way to their promised land.

Thus we pushed our way eventually into the primeval heat of the immemorial Indian Ocean.

15

BOHUNICKY, the Bohunk, our bosun, had died frightfully in the very hour of our passing from the Red Sea, of hydrophobia. Ironically he died in pathological abhorrence of the water he had always dreaded, the mad dog he had feared he might be, having taken the only precautions against madness he knew.

The day after Simms and I had gone ashore at Port Said Simms had sought out the Bohunk and advised that he get a doctor to treat him for the bite. Never having been treated by a doctor in his life the Bohunk had grunted and said he had had worse sores from scratching lice. Until the diagnosis of rabies by the uncanny steward no one had thought again of the episode of the dogfight. By then there was no recourse.

Even before we made our entrance to the great ditch everybody had begun to take less and less notice of anybody else. Subsequently there were remembered, and by more than one, various signs and symptoms, not so much of abnormality as of exaggerated normality. The Bohunk had sat out a vigil on the grating of the second level of the engine room, his back against the ladder, in a sheen of sweat, while the machinery pounding all around him like a rolling mill vibrated and reverberated in his head till he appeared lulled into a catatonic peace. He had lain bathing in the noise as on a warm beach hour upon hour, with a look of beatitude on his usually taut face, like a music-lover whose sense floats upon the movement of a symphony. If he was in the way, that had not been cared about. Now and again a shout by anyone ascending or descending the ladder at whose base he sprawled had gone unheard, a prodding foot unfelt.

In the mess hall he had been withdrawn and off his feed, more than the rest of us in the poisonous heat, responding if at all with alternating irritability and lethargy, peevishly brooding so it had seemed on the mystique of din below deck, where exaltation stood him for sleep.

I was in the crews' mess the noon he went berserk. I happened to be looking when his friend Frenchy, sitting beside him, had filled his own glass with water, turned and filled Bohunicky's. I saw the water spill over the table, and the muscles of the Bohunk's neck, square and hard as an iron ingot, contracting as though he retched. A second later with his grotesque ape-like grace he had been on his feet and had taken Frenchy by the throat.

During the initial interval of his surprise Frenchy had been inert, but as the Bohunk bent him in his throttling grip viciously backward over the edge of the table, he had writhed and flailed in silent frenzy. Tough as the pulp logs he had once cut six to eight cords of a day, Frenchy had been impotent as a child in that choking clutch, but it was some moments before the men understood that he was being strangled.

Parsons, the giant Georgian, was the first to jump to his feet, yelling, "Bunk — lay off — what the hell ails yeh!" He had then tried to separate the two by getting his arm around the Bohunk's neck from behind. But the Bohunk dug his chin into his chest and when he was heaved backward carried the suffocating Frenchy with him. As others piled on him he had dropped Frenchy, who staggered in a little circle and fell gasping face down across the table, where he lay in the midst and on top of soiled dishes.

They got the Bohunk down, but it had been like getting a grizzly bear on his back, they couldn't do anything with him. He fought his way to his feet gutturally snarling. One man was dashed to the bulkhead, against which he had then leaned momentarily with an expression of luxurious comfort till his knees sagged and slowly, almost laughably, he slid down as though he were stooping arthritically to pick some nonexistent object off the deck.

Having heard the crashing dishes and the explosive half-shouts Simms had appeared just as Sparks was circling the reeling, plunging, heaving group, a spanner wrench in hand, trying to land a strategic blow on the Bohunk's iron skull. When Simms grabbed the wrench Sparks had cried, "He's run amuck!"

Simms had then held out his key ring by one key and told the steward to get a Syrette. Next he ordered the men to let Bohunicky loose before somebody got killed. They hesitated, dubious. "Somebody's liable to if we do," Parsons warned. But when Simms repeated his order they stepped warily aside.

"Keep cool, Bohunicky," Simms had placatingly said, as the Bohunk, free, gulping his breath with a sound almost like barking, confronted him with a quartzy stare. Simms had had his nerve with him. "You'll be all right. It's the heat."

Just as it had seemed that the Bohunk would indeed calm down he made a lightning silent lunge at Simms and the expectant men were on him again, swaying and lurching. Over the deadly scuffing of their feet on the deck Simms had said once more, "Let him loose."

The steward was back and this time I saw with amazement the great round tears running down the Bohunk's hairy spatulate cheeks. "Help me —" He was choking. "Help me —"

"That's what we're doing," Simms had explained, tearing

at the Syrette the steward had brought. "This is going to help you get some sleep. You need to sleep." And stepping forward he had squeezed the entire contents of the tube into the Bohunk's biceps.

Bohunicky had stood choking, and sobbing out, "Help me — help me — help me —" Then in a flash he had leaped at Simms, and the tensed men grappled with him again and went down on the deck, and stepping back Simms had said, "Hang onto him a minute — he's got enough morphine in him to knock a horse out."

Once he lay quietly on his back rasping in his throat, the men standing around him breathless and dismayed, Simms and the steward had bent over him. "I don't know if it's the proper treatment," Simms said, "but at least it'll keep him for a while from killing himself or someone else."

It was immediately afterward that the steward had said with incontrovertible authority, "Rabies — he's got rabies."

Evasively, one after another, the crew had disappeared from the mess hall, leaving, besides Simms, the steward, and Bohunicky on the deck, only Parsons looming staunch and solid and Frenchy semiconscious on the table.

The next night, roped to his bunk, with hoarse gagging yelps and great wracking convulsions, Bohunicky had died.

We had taken him to be without the ordinary fragility of body. He had stayed on the job, his voice booming out of his inexhaustible lungs, his cropped projectile-shaped head thrusting about the ship, forty-eight hours at a stretch when necessary, without weariness. He had never been seasick, or any other kind of sick. He had seemed physically as invulnerable as stone. Now, in a way that curiously eluded the help he had begged us to give him and that we would have given him if we could, in a way that would have perplexed him thoroughly, he had been struck dead through a clandestine and unerring certainty. While we, deprived of the simple witness of his flesh and mind, felt in contrast the shock of our complex helplessness.

The Old Man's behavior when he was notified in the morning had upset us further. He was lying on his bunk when Simms told him, gazing at the overhead, and had responded only by closing his blank eyes. Toward the middle of the afternoon he had called the steward and ordered him to have the body laid out in the saloon. Two hours later just before suppertime he had stepped unsteadily into the saloon and stood for several minutes staring down on Bohunicky's body as though studying the face of death in search of something familiar that he would recognize.

After supper word was passed that the Old Man had ordered the corpse sewn up in canvas and weighted for burial at sea. Sayles particularly was confused, and he had gone, taking Simms with him for support, and asked the Old Man why we did not keep Bohunicky under refrigeration till we reached port, as we had the gunners who were killed at Anzio. At that time the Old Man had in fact said it was not his policy to bury men at sea unless it was absolutely necessary. When the Old Man did not answer him even in any way Sayles had stared a while at his feet, and rubbing his solidal frown had closed the door of the Old Man's stateroom and gone away preposterously on tiptoe.

At noon the following day the ship was stopped. We hove to in vivid sunlight and a molten calm on which our wake had been a living scar. Frenchy and Parsons had then come out of the crews' quarters by the after door each carrying one end of a plank on which the body of Bohunicky rested in its canvas envelope like a monstrous cocoon. They showed a little that they had been drinking the night away.

The whole orbiting globe seemed to lay to for the occasion in its own haze. The Old Man had come out, taken several steps weakly and softly onto the open deck, drawn himself erect with his head bare and slightly palsied in the blatant sunshine, and begun almost at once to read in sepulchral tones from a prayer book with a broken binding. . . . *though he were dead, yet shall he live . . .*

In his great trembling hand the loose leaves of the prayer book fluttered in the breathless air . . . *though after my skin worms destroy this body* . . . Behind him the mates had come on deck together while he read. . . . *let me know mine end, and the number of my days that I may be certified how long I have to live.* . . . Frenchy had rested on the bulwark the forward end of the plank bearing the feet of Bohunicky's body and shuffled back alongside Parsons. They had faced one another without meeting each other's eyes, supporting the inboard end of the plank, and Frenchy's wiry neck glowed black with bruises. . . . *mine age is even as nothing.* . . . The Old Man read in a quavering voice. One by one five of the black gang, bearded and oil-stained, had trickled through the door and ranged in a restless shuffling semicircle near the radiant bulkhead. Finally the steward emerged and glanced around with his fermenting gaze. No one else appeared.

Attestingly the Old Man's voice, having sunk into a feeble rattle, had boomed out with old vigor upon that utterly quiescent day. . . . *O spare me a little, that I may recover my strength before I go hence and be no more seen.* . . . Frenchy and Parsons swayed together in gentle unison moving the head of the plank so that the foot of it scraped and creaked on the rail. . . . *The days of our age are threescore years and ten and though men be so strong that they come to fourscore years yet is their strength then but labor and sorrow so soon passeth it away and we are gone.* . . .

Parsons, snapping his head over his shoulder then, had hissed, "The flag —" No one had remembered this crucial formality. Moving behind the men I went topside and found, rummaging in the flag box, a tattered and faded ensign which was not much more dilapidated than the one we had been flying. I took it circuitously back and reaching the head of the plank flipped it out so that it settled like gossamer a trifle askew over the canvas sack. The Old Man had read on meanwhile. . . . *So when this corruption shall have put on incorruption, and this mortality shall have put on immortality, then shall be brought to pass the saying that is written, Death is swallowed up in victory. . . .*

"Should be fastened—" Parsons had said in a rasping whisper.

And I back, "You'll have to hold it."

Man that is born of a woman hath but a short time to live, and is full of misery . . . he fleeth as it were a shadow, and never continueth in one stay. . . . I had withdrawn as Parsons and Frenchy fumbled to pin the edges of the ensign under their thumbs.

In the midst of life we are in death. . . .

The Old Man's intonation rumbled hollowly like distant shifting ice. He licked his purple lips. . . . *We therefore commit his body to the deep. . . .* He looked up for the first time into the shadowless day, straight ahead with watery gaze, a fine dew gathering on the old pallor of his forehead.

Parsons and Frenchy shoved the plank part way over the rail and raised their end. But the white sunlit bundle failed to slide vertically. Instead, appallingly, it had rolled sideways off the plank taking the ensign with it. . . . *the sea shall give up her dead; and the corruptible bodies of those who sleep in him shall be changed. . . .*

Parsons and Frenchy had faced each other, arms aloft, holding the raised end of the tilted plank as though in the act of playing "London-Bridge-Is-Falling-Down," while their shipmate, wound in red-white-and-blue bunting, had spun downward like a bizarre Oriental top, and the imponderable ocean of India had swallowed his tiny freakish swirl forever in a single quicksilvery laugh.

16

THOUGH I had a third officer's papers, my billet was a seaman's and my watches consisted occasionally of manning the radar but chiefly of steering assigned courses. My personal routine was worked out almost exclusively between the wheelhouse and my lifeboat, which came to represent a sanctuary where all was in universal heat around me.

The deterioration taking place in shipboard discipline was now without camouflage or pretext. Simms and even the conscientious Sayles committed the unpardonable sin of not relieving the watch promptly. The first time this happened to O'Hara he raised hell with both of them. In the face of his onslaught Simms, with lowered head, kept dully silent. But Sayles, with a fanatical gleam in his eyes, waited O'Hara out and then said: "This ain't yore ship yet."

Once again O'Hara appeared disconcerted by this implication from Sayles. "The Old Man is sick," he replied. "He's not fit."

Sayles canted his head quizzically. "I say it's his ship."

"He can't run it," O'Hara said. "I am responsible."

"It's still his ship," Sayles insisted. "We don't want yew to be responsible. Soon or late someday like him yew'll git old an' die." And with an unpleasant leer he added, "It ain't yore world 'ny more 'n it is his, or no one's." There was something elusively mutinous in his delivery of this pious truism.

O'Hara's face flushed, a blood vessel in his temple throbbed. "You're wrong, Mister," he said. "The whole world may not be mine. But the space of it I'm in — my part of it — is. It may not be for sure, or for much, or for long. But while I'm in it, it'll know me."

Thereafter O'Hara was relieved on time. But he was the only one, and oddly enough he began to pay no attention to what went on apart from his particular movements.

Sometimes the relief watch would not appear for an hour or more. The second, if not relieved, would steer while the helmsman went in search of the relief, or he would wander out after him himself. For long periods there might be no officer on the bridge and only a helmsman in the wheelhouse. Simms, to whom navigation had once been a sport that he had gladly taken over from Sayles, who was made nervous by it, seldom showed for morning sights. He would come up at noon for a sun line, tan, hairy, and glistening, in his underwear.

"Christ — what a sun!" he would exclaim, squinting through the colored glass of his sextant while the sweat poured into his eyes. "Hove to, right at the zenith." It became his stock and automatic response to every sun, which glowed through the polaroid screens of his sextant like the yellowish-green unshadowed eye of a cat.

At evening startime he would halfheartedly amble around the bridge, sextant in hand, still in his underwear, doodle a few minutes with lines of position on the plotting sheet, trying to make out the critical little triangle of a fix which would give him the *Belle's* position, throw down his pencil and say, "Too smoky — no horizon! How in hell am I supposed to know where we are? Have those goddamn chronometers been wound?" Then he would grab a piece of paper, jot down a longitude and latitude, and go below, saying, "Here — log this. Might as well be here as anywhere."

But he was usually on deck for the evening watch punctually at twenty-hundred because the Old Man was now able occasionally to sit for a spell on his bridge in the deep equatorial dark. The Old Man's battle with his body was certainly heroic and, like the sentiment of heroism itself, outside the aspect of eternity as certainly pointless and futile. It was as if all the ills that flesh is heir to had given him this final challenge, and his doughty spirit had taken it up from long habit and in order not to fail its former victories.

He had formerly regulated his habits by a kind of time which for lack of a more suitable word I will have to call moral. Everything he did, whether executive, operational, or merely personal, was according to this strangely ethical prompting. It was almost a point of honor with him to be on his bridge every morning from oh-six-hundred to oh-eight-hundred and every evening from nineteen-hundred to twenty-one-hundred regardless of what was going on or how much sleep he had had. We never had to call him at these hours, or notify him when they were past, though he kept his watch in his wall safe. We simply expected him through an automatic reflex of our own.

Apparently he had lived this way so long his very body functioned synchronously with it. If he ordered a course or speed change for the middle of the night he would be awake when it was made, and if we failed by thirty seconds to make it promptly we knew positively we would hear from him. We braced to hear from him also within seconds whenever there was any unscheduled change in the ship's rhythms, a marked alteration in her turns or her course, a shift of wind or rising of sea, a failure of the engineers to blow tubes one half-hour after nightfall, an increase of vibration from mechanical trouble. Thus exquisitely had his physical being been tuned to his official one.

Now as one after the other these certitudes slipped from

our lives, we adjusted to the insecurity of their absence by growing lax ourselves and losing our own dependable peculiarities of behavior. Sparks's fingers, for example, which we had grown accustomed to see bleeding where he had chewed his nails down into the sensitive flesh, began to sprout nails that showed semicircles of grime under long, untrimmed edges. As though it had been erased by constant rubbing Sayles's virgular scowl had faded to a faint line and appeared not to aggravate him any more since he ceased to rub it altogether. Little differences like these were evidence of a strange and progressive serenity. They were symptoms of the East, and indicated that already it was seeping into our flesh, pacifying our bones, liquefying our bowels, vaporizing our brains.

Eventually and perceptibly Captain Blake changed from the old mariner unwilling to grant the merchant marine or any reality, including the ageless sea itself, a longevity apart from or superior to his individual cognizance. He now sat in his chair seeming to stare across crepuscular distances without horizons, distances no one else saw, facing the phenomena of an uninhabited and uninhabitable world of planes and surfaces no one else imagined. Once in a while he would inquire huskily what course and speed we were making good, and when he was informed would nod profoundly in the manner of one voyaging to the moon in a capsule, where motion consisted not of tangibles susceptible to management but of data that could only be noted.

It was impossible to suppose he was any more afraid of death than he had ever been, or, if he had had his choice, he would not have joined with it quickly in action as he had with life. By virtue of being sick, and probably dying, on a schedule unrelated to anything we knew or were doing, he seemed to us to have shed his familiar personal dimension and taken on an estranging, alien, immaterial one. Instead of a man he had become, sitting motionlessly aloft absorbed in the night, or shut silently up in his cabin, a kind of mere presence — of something without memory or prolepsis, regret or hope — that belonged neither to the next world nor this, but to a dreadful interim exclusively its own.

This helped explain the callousness, mounting to resentment, toward his illness on the part of men some of whom had loved him and perhaps still did, and all of whom owed their lives to him. If he died they would doubtless have accorded him their transient grief and gone their ways with the lives he had saved for them as if the living of these was as much a matter of course as the dwindling of his. But his present condition, like an oppressive and tyrannical office, seemed to remind them of something hateful which they had to identify with him personally. No flag officer could have been so unapproachable. Even O'Hara spoke to him as seldom and shortly as he could, and then in a pained undertone you could hardly hear.

I took to brooding over whether the sense of annihilation, of the important self forever blotted out while mankind pursued whatever ends, any ends, without you, was more fearful before you had had your life, as surely the Old Man had. The acute imagination would unexpectedly electrify me with horror as I went mechanically about my functions, so that a frenzy of haste rose in me and I wanted to tear at the bars of this captivity which kept me from my promise. If this occurred during my watch I would cling weak and nauseated to the wheel until my relief came, when I would retreat to my lifeboat to lie for hours in a state of nervous exhaustion. If it came upon me there I would rush out and about the decks in a condition of hypermotility. I was certain everyone must see that something was the matter with me. But not a soul noticed.

My relief helmsmen, never on time, had the habit when coming on watch of asking at the very bottom of a sigh, as if they needed to keep their breath for something besides talk, "Where in hell are we?" Then they would go and pore over the chart table, while the salt sweat dropping off the ends of their noses and chins splashed into the Indian Ocean, white and blank and extending out of plotting reach off the limiting edges of the charted world they could not interpret. In the past the mate on watch used to put a finger on the ship's dead reckoning position. Now if he happened to be on deck, he merely growled, "What's it to you?" if he said anything.

Out there there was no beginning, middle, or end to anything, and hardly anything. Everything there was was insubstantial and the same. It was like at once the dawn of creation and the dusk of annihilation, a frontier, a frontier recedent and pointless, leading nowhere and to nothing, undevelopable, a verge that would always be, never be anything but, verge.

Nobody spoke more than he had to, and less than he should have for the management of the ship, so that we were enveloped in a hot womb-like silence where communication was by a kind of latent primal instinct similar to the understanding between men guilty of a mutual crime. Speech was superfluous.

Fortunately we were not menaced by bad weather. It was the season of the rainy southwest monsoon, but no wind blew and no rain fell. Only an infrequent squall gusted over the flat sea like the shadow of some prehistoric bird. We stuck straight up off the bare round planet, not so much as a shade anywhere to shelter us from the crushing heat and flawless universal sunlight. The air trembled liquidly as if it were a highly volatile and combustible gas heated to the flash point. Our flaccid wake, dangling from the rim of the unbearable heavens, seemed to suspend us by our stern pendulous and still above an aqueous void. The sheet of water was bleached as white in the implacable sun as that nothingness which the chart diagrammed in rectangular sections with thinly visible lines of longitude and latitude, and which it plumbed the hidden dimensions of by mysterious numbers as in a geodetic lottery, translating the impalpable depths and

121

curvatures of the creation into abstract mathematical symbols. What did we care for those invisible hills and vales, those ranges of mountain peaks towering below us, looming up numerically beneath our frail substantial keel?

Going off watch one evening I went directly to my lifeboat as my custom was, and stretched out on my mattress gazing up at the dim unfamiliar stars. The Old Man was on the bridge when I left, but Simms had not arrived. I knew where he was because I had seen him through the open door of the chief engineer's stateroom. I lolled on my back, I hardly realized how long, not being able to sleep. Then instantaneously the vibrations transmitted by the ship's engine and shaft through the davits to my lifeboat stopped, the ship fell silent, and I knew that all she had left was the inertia carrying her into her dying momentum. Without the noise and tremor of her engine she lost at once her identity and became a mere pocket of the tropical night. In near panic, before I thought, I had scrambled from my sanctuary and hurried to the wheelhouse. O'Hara was stomping up the ladder. He took a quick glance at the engine-room telegraph and barked, "What's going on?" He had been for several days bristling with an eruption of prickly heat all over his face and neck, and now, having plastered himself with calomine lotion, he glowed in the light of the wheelhouse as though he were wearing a luminous mask.

"That Simms has been tyin' one on with Costello," the man at the wheel replied in a moody undertone. "When he come on watch boiled, the Old Man caught it an' kicked him off duty."

"But the main propulsion's gone," said O'Hara.

"Yah," said the helmsman. Realizing for the first time that he was holding a useless wheel he turned around, leaned back against it, and lit a cigarette. "Simms goes below an' Costello sees him an' comes up plastered an' tells the Old Man everybody topside don't amount to a good oiler anyway, an' if Simms don't go on watch he cuts the goddamn engine. The

122

Old Man yells he ain't havin' no officer that's been drinkin' on his bridge." The helmsman blew out a hissing stream of smoke in indiscriminate disgust. It broke and billowed on the air between him and O'Hara, who had an ascetic dislike of tobacco and took a backward step. "Costello says Simms is able enough an' the best he's got an' he'll put him on watch or he won't push this honey-barge another mile. The Old Man tells Costello he'll put him ashore on a mutiny charge, an' Costello tells him he won't never make port if that's the way it is. So the Old Man yells he'll have Costello in the brig, an' Costello fetches the great leap down the passageway and goes below."

O'Hara heard the helmsman out and went up to the bridge. Through the voice tube we heard him speaking in his rasping monotone, then we heard the Old Man's voice, booming, quavering from short-windedness, but unfailingly authoritative.

"Mr. O'Hara — I will not have an officer — who's been drinking — on my bridge! You know my policies."

O'Hara said something we could not get through the tube.

"Put the chief engineer under arrest — confine him to quarters!" the Old Man bellowed with surprising strength.

Vaguely O'Hara said, "I'll see what I can do."

"You will do — as I order —" the Old Man blurted.

O'Hara was gone a long time, during which I walked out onto the starboard wing into the black heat, and the helmsman, leaning against the wheel, smoked a series of cigarettes. When O'Hara finally returned and went up to the Old Man I stayed where I was, listening.

"The engineers won't go down without Costello's say-so," I heard O'Hara over my head flatly announce. "I've therefore told Simms to stand his watch. He's able enough."

This was an astonishing and untoward move even for Costello, this gratuitous, inappropriate assertion of his disgruntlement, his disaffection and loss of confidence. The Old

123

Man's and O'Hara's inability to meet it for whatever reasons was equally unsettling. It was, all round, a dangerous political failure.

Not a sound came from the bridge. I waited with great misgiving an indeterminate interval, when abruptly the ship began to vibrate again. The helmsman reversed himself and spun the wheel.

"Mr. O'Hara —" We heard the Old Man's cry, frail and hollow out of the darkness. There was immediately the thump of something heavy softly falling on the steel plating overhead.

"One of you there — lend a hand," O'Hara called down through the tube.

I climbed to the bridge and saw the Old Man sprawled on deck like a fragment from the night. O'Hara stared me in the eye. "He fell," he explained tersely. "Take his feet."

We had our trouble getting the Old Man to his cabin. He seemed unconscious and breathed so shallowly I couldn't be sure he was not dead. Emaciated though he was, he was a tremendous burden, awkwardly long, and his bones felt like oak sticks. We lowered him down. His arms kept catching as though even insensible he refused to leave his post.

O'Hara kicked open the door to the Old Man's stateroom and switched on the light. While we were preparing to lift him inside he came to enough to get his feet under him. Throwing us both back convulsively with a thrust of his gangling arms he reeled across the floor and dropped to his knees against the side of his bunk, his horny elbows dug into the bedding, his head bowed.

I caught a glimpse of O'Hara's pink chalked face. It revealed mortal embarrassment. Then it dawned on me — he expected the Old Man was going to pray. He half turned toward me in a way that made me suppose he would have got out if I had not been standing between him and the door. I was for him a trivial and far from immovable obstacle and I actually felt myself already shoved aside by his will, but for the moment I proved, in the peculiar balance of mood and circumstance, enough.

We stood together behind the Old Man, the skeletal outline of his enormous bone structure morbidly outlined beneath his sweaty yellow undershirt, wisps of pale yellow hair straggling over his white and vulnerable skull. We heard him whispering to himself, terrifyingly feeble and fierce in the still room which smelled of age and death.

"I damn —" the Old Man hissed in spent fury. His entire body shook, the palsied craggy head worse than the rest. "I damn this corruption — in the flesh — in the mind. . . ."

With that he collapsed and we gingerly, as if he might momentarily rise up like a martyr from the fire, laid the rack of that wasted old Titan in its bed, and left it with the light out and the door closed.

17

FOR SEVERAL DAYS after this incident I suffered increasingly from the delusion that a rank odor of some sort enveloped my lifeboat. At first it was so insidious that I vaguely wondered if I were not perhaps hallucinated. When it grew more pronounced I aired my bedding and clothes, attributing it to the atmosphere that permeated and made fetid everything. And when it became daily stronger and more vile I would leap up at frequent intervals to ransack my lifeboat as you would hunt for the carcass of a rat that had died in the partitions.

It had to come, I reasoned, from some decaying organism, it was that putrid. I went sniffing over the same places again and again, through the bilges, behind the water casks, in the lockers, underneath the gear, till I fell back on my mattress in confusion. I even suspected my own body, and tried to smell my breath by cupping my hand over my mouth and nose in an effort to breathe out and inhale at the same time. But the stench hovered about the lifeboat like an invisible cloud. Being unable to locate its source I developed an acute anxiety in which I began to suspect some rare disorder of my senses.

Then one morning I awoke to discover that I was breathing in air so foul that I was more than nauseated, I was frightened. My skin chilled with revulsion. I tried not to breathe while I struggled in desperate haste into my trousers and sneakers. By the time I hit the deck the pulses were crashing in my temples and my brain was a furnace. When I finally had to draw breath the fearful stench struck me in the face like a flame.

In the irrational urge for refuge I rushed inside and slammed the door behind me. For a moment by contrast the air smelled sweet and clean, but as I leaned against the bulkhead to regain my breathing the odor reasserted itself, though very faintly. On sheer impulse born of desperation I threw open the door of the fiddley and felt the hot upward blast ventilating the engine room. There on the metal grill between the outer shell and the smokestack, where we hung our oilskins to dry quickly in bad weather, lay a charred object. It was as black as charcoal, but unmistakably it was what it was.

I flung back the door and ran out across the boat deck to the rail. As soon as I was able I drove myself back inside to O'Hara's cabin, bursting through the door without knocking. He was lying on his back in his bunk, stark naked, with his eyes open. There was a bottle and a roll of cotton batting on the desk within his reach, and the immaculate cabin was full of the fumes of carbolic acid, like the room where a corpse has been laid out.

In slow amazement O'Hara swung his feet onto the floor and stared at me. I saw that he was caked all over with chalk from the dried calomine lotion, through which prickled the red rash and red hair on his body, and the blood raging into his thick neck and face. He looked like a firebrand.

"You son of a bitch!" he yelled. "Get out of here!"

"There's a man in the fiddley —" I yelled back.

"Get —" He lunged to his feet and made for me.

"Dead!" I shouted at him, retreating through the door.

I backed out into the passageway and O'Hara stopped inside the door trying to focus his bloodshot eyes. "In the fiddley?" he repeated at last, thickly.

"Cooked!" I exclaimed. "Burnt to a crisp."

After another pause he said, "Who?"

"I couldn't tell," I told him. "He's unrecognizable."

I went outside to the rail again, overcome by the mere recollection of those unidentifiable features burnt into their grimace of agony.

As I returned O'Hara strode past me in his drawers and slippers. He was built compactly like a bullock, and he put his feet down as though they were more solid than the deck he walked on. In spite of conditions I was intrigued to note the design which decorated his shorts — large red and yellow hubs, spokes, and rims with the legend sprinkled round them at angles in blue letters, "Big Wheel — Big Wheel — Big Wheel," obviously someone's gift to him for a joke.

He opened the fiddley door and leaned well in. Then he swung back, closed the door, and returned with the same solid tread to where I was.

"Tell Parsons to spread a tarp and shovel him up," he said. "It's the only way he'll get him over the side. And tell him to take a muster." He entered his cabin and shut his door upon the smell of that astounding disinfectant.

I did what I was told, then I went to the wheelhouse because it was my watch. The helmsman going off was alone there. To relieve my horror and perhaps my curiosity I told him what had happened. He leaned against the log desk watching me brightly but, I thought, queerly without surprise. I trailed off, saying, "Who — which one of us . . . ?"

He scratched his untrimmed beard; everyone aboard except the Old Man, the steward, who shaved him, O'Hara, who had prickly heat, and me, had quit shaving.

"Sparks most likely."

"Why Sparks?"

"Buddy of Armpit's. Nobody seen him lately."

The extended absence of a member of a small, close ship's company, whom his shipmates several times a day every day were accustomed to seeing, had gone half-acknowledged and uninvestigated. I pondered this, and screwed myself to ask him the unavoidable but probably unanswerable question. "What would Sparks be doing in the fiddley?" I did not expect the man I was relieving to give me a fact but to help me speculate.

He shot me a weird glance. "The monkey got him."

"The monkey —"

As he started aft through the passageway he added, enigmatically as if he were making a macabre, cryptic witticism, "That monkey'll likely get a few more before long."

He sounded a little crazy, I preferred to think.

By noon when I went off watch it was known by its dog tags that the baked, decomposing body in the fiddley had been the radio operator. They had sunk the remains in a canvas sack without funeral rites.

Once more I could curl safely, fetally in my lifeboat.

But that was not quite all there was to it, because, while the air was breathable and no longer threatened my security, something else did — a debilitating sense of contamination that was not to be registered through my nostrils. I hated to recognize the source of that terrible stench as burning human flesh, which in being tried seemed to disclose a concealed impurity, putrid beyond belief beside the fine sharp tang of searing beef. It had smelled like all the unwashed stinking feet in the world!

Come eight o'clock I was glad to go on watch again for the purifying, almost religious ritual of rolling the wheel and narrowing my concentration to the compass card floating, an iridescent pinprick of certainty, above the formless inky water.

The radio shack was unmanned. The books on electronics remained arranged on the shelves where Sparks had neglected them for his pernicious peace of mind and nerves, the earphones through which his brain had traversed the squeaking ether and the key on which he responded with torn fingertips and muffled concentration lay on the console. It was not easy to forget, withdrawn though he had always been, the distraught albino gaze of his split consciousness as, slipping a phone off one ear and tilting his face wistfully toward you in the doorway, he gave you his divided attention. The room remained empty, with the door insinuatingly open, as though communication was no more necessary than this single little man.

The *Belle* in fact had reached a point of hardly being manned at all. Apart from my schedule, which I stuck to, there was no observable sequence of wheel watches. The man you relieved or who relieved you was seldom the same. Your relief might show up anywhere from a half-hour to two hours late, and offering no explanation or excuse silently take the wheel and fall to steering the course you gave him. One midwatch the helmsman having been drinking had fallen asleep over the wheel, and by the time his tardy relief arrived the *Belle* had strayed a hundred and twenty degrees from course, and no one the wiser in the night. I suspected the crew drew lots or played poker to see who would take the duty. I did not know, nor did I ask, who or what drove them on watch at all, and I tried not to think of a watch when I might be abandoned at the wheel altogether.

This night at startime the third passed through his motions of obtaining a fix, logged his estimate of the ship's position himself, and retired without having muttered a syllable. Though our track on the chart did not indicate so, it had occurred to me we must have been cruising well outside any shipping lanes, since we had not sighted another vessel in several days, and a fleeting ambition to obtain a fix myself at morning startime, which Simms now habitually slept through, lingered like a dissolving shadow in my mind. I did nothing, from fear of what I might discover and from doubt of what I might do about it.

Left alone I fell to worrying the riddle — what was Sparks's body doing in the fiddley? If he had been murdered why hadn't whoever did it thrown him overboard? On the other hand, why would he have gone there of his own will? He was never on the weather decks long enough to get his clothes wet, and we had only had a few afternoon squalls. In this climate the fiddley was a blast furnace. But there he was, found by me, and the fact was as disquieting as if the chain of cause and effect had snapped and things were revealed to be in truth connected only according to some underlying irrationality.

I was jostled in the midst of this quandary by O'Hara entering the wheelhouse in his slippers and pajama bottoms. Even before I heard him I was warned of his arrival by the smell of that antiseptic phenol. His rash had worsened and now flared through the fresh dry layer of chalk with which he had tried to soothe himself. As though no one but him was left on the entire ship he took a position just outside the wheelhouse on the starboard wing, where in her slow progress the *Belle* voluptuously created, in the dead night everywhere else, her own little island of faint breeze.

Thus he soothed his flaming flesh, and for an hour or more thus I steered, uneasy in the unacknowledged company of this allergic man.

He must have come into the wheelhouse behind me from his cabin. But how long he had been examining the compass over my shoulder I could never testify. I did not hear or see him until the moment I heard his hoarse order to turn the ship about. He stood at my back, fully clothed in his uniform, pallor on his cliff of a face, a wild energy glinting in his clouded eyes, and an automatic pistol in his right hand.

"Skipper — what's up?" O'Hara was now a few feet inside the wheelhouse eying the Old Man's uniform and the automatic.

The Old Man whirled with surprising force and thundered, "Where are you taking my ship, Mr. O'Hara? This is not the course to Gibraltar! Why have you dropped out of convoy? Do you want us sunk? Give me a range and bearing —" he filled his laboring lungs — "to the guide!"

O'Hara hesitated, alert. "The ship is not going to Gibraltar," he replied, watching the Old Man guardedly. "There is no guide."

The Old Man took a long stride toward his chief mate. "I am master here —" he threatened. "This vessel will steam where she is directed." With a disagreeable and wholly uncharacteristic gleam of cunning he added, "Because I have been sick you think I don't know what has been going on!"

I saw O'Hara's glance waver a second. Then he said in his matter-of-fact monotone, "The ship is heading for Freemantle."

"Helmsman —" the Old Man raged, "put her about!"

"Hold your course," O'Hara told me, a tremor in his voice. "He doesn't even know what ocean he's in."

At that the Old Man raised his arm and attempted to point the automatic squarely at O'Hara. "There will be no sneaking mutiny while I am in command!" His voice had a raving quality and his eyes glittered abnormally.

"Stop the engine!" he cried out. It was a remarkable resurgence of energy, but it had no reserve. "I will give you one more order. Stop the engine —"

The automatic began to wobble from side to side and up and down at the end of the Old Man's long arm. O'Hara noted this and flexed himself. The Old Man saw it also, stared briefly at the automatic as though it were being clutched in somebody else's hand, then suddenly dashed it to the deck where it struck with a shocking clang and went skittering against the bulkhead.

"I need no weapon —" the Old Man gasped. He went for O'Hara with his horny fists clenched so that the knuckles stuck out like spurs.

"You're out of your head," O'Hara told him quickly. "The

132

war is over." He had always been a brave man, and he did not exactly show fear now. Yet he balanced himself carefully, for there was something to beware in the Old Man's stance, as of a wrathful if dispossessed deity, and in his unhealthy burst of energy, as of a generator winding into a high whine seconds before it lets go.

Suddenly the Old Man swung widely at O'Hara's head. O'Hara did not raise a hand. But he stepped back. The Old Man's great arm flailed through the air, and striking nothing threw him off his staggering balance. On his face was an expression of vast astonishment and disbelief that his body had repudiated his will. He tottered a dreadful instant and toppled to the deck like a tall mast. His cap rolled round and round, decelerating like an enormous gold coin, and flopped to a standstill by his feet.

O'Hara, after following the cap with his eyes till it came to rest, bent above the Old Man as though to raise his giant husk from the deck and sustain it in his own muscular embrace. But some kind of morbid spell seemed cast on him by the Old Man's dissolution. For the first time I was seeing him incapable of action, his shoulders and head bowed in agonizing impotence. The Old Man was not unconscious, but he was not aware — the victim of his age which alone had been able to return him to the younger vigorous life it had worn away. He lay without struggling and raved in a moaning voice.

It was not pitiful or pitiable, it was awesome, terrifying, so that I quaked incurably. With a flinching twist of his whole being O'Hara disappeared into the passageway, leaving me alone with the Old Man lying on the deck breathing his incoherent moans. And I knew that so long as I lived I was going to be haunted by the memory of that spectral image felled in the soft twilight of its pilothouse.

O'Hara returned with two crewmen in tow, both drunk, who fetched up unsteadily at sight of the Old Man stretched on the deck.

"Chrishake — it's theshkipper!" one said. They stood and swayed together foggily.

"Get him back to his bed," O'Hara said harshly, his face averted.

"Ain' daid," said the seaman.

"Pre'y fur gone —" said his companion. He stooped and picked up the Old Man's cap and placed it on his own head, the visor with its gold braid in back. "Whew —" He pinched his nose with thumb and finger. "Mussuv messtmself —"

O'Hara extended his hand. "I'll take the cap." His voice grated.

While they were sliding and grunting over their burden he had his back turned, the Old Man's cap hanging from one hand, and faced toward the wing out into the night. It struck me with surprise, because it was so out of character, that he could not bear to watch.

One of the seamen tugging at the Old Man grunted, "Ain' ee the ol' baster though."

"Ol' baster," said the other.

Finally as they moved into the passageway O'Hara said, "Lock the cabin and take the steward the key."

Afterward he stepped out on the wing a way. I could see him in the semi-darkness, dimly lit by light from the wheel-house, turning the Old Man's cap over and over in his red-haired hands till I wondered if he were contemplating putting it on his own head. But he did not.

Now, I thought, he had his command. He was the Old Man at last through this wretched default, and I waited to see what would be his first move.

He must have stayed that way, twisting the Old Man's cap, maybe a quarter of an hour. I supposed he was getting adjusted to the responsibility he must at times have thought — must at times even been guilty of hoping — might come to him in some such manner as this. When he came back into the light wearing his pajama pants he glanced about, the cap still in both hands, like a man who had been long in the

134

dark, long absent from the familiar and known. His face seemed to have grown in a matter of minutes the age lines of a decade. His ghostly mask of chalk gave him the abstracted look of a clown falling through thin air. His eyes were puffy and clouded the same as the Old Man's. He swayed as if for a moment he might be going to measure his own length on the wheelhouse deck, though the ship was as firm as cement. The antiseptic odor of phenol still clung to him.

Under his breath he said, "Stop the engine."

"Stop —" I was flabbergasted. I hung there not knowing whether to believe him or not.

But he was no joker. Barely audible this time he repeated himself. "Stop the engine. You heard the captain —"

I might have expected mutiny from O'Hara, but not this. Or was this a subtler form of mutiny? Was he out of his mind too? It was the first and last ambiguous thing I ever knew him to do. Something, almost I thought like sentiment, had betrayed the integrity of his nature. Was he unnerved by the status he had always wanted now that he had it? His personality seemed to have faltered from a new strange confusion — or was it clarity?

After a few seconds, unable to match his gaze with my baffled one, I reached for the annunciator, jerked the handle, and listened to the bells jangle late obedience to a command tortuously formulated in the misconceptions of a tormented old man.

I may have held my breath till I felt the Belle's vibrations finally die. At any rate I was short of wind once we settled into our inertia.

The engine room rang the wheelhouse. Over the phone a subliminal voice said vaguely, "What goes on?"

"Mr. O'Hara's orders," I said into the phone.

"Captain's order!" O'Hara's sharp hiss corrected me.

"What's wrong?" the disinterested voice inquired from below.

"I don't know," I answered shakily, and I didn't. "Captain's order."

"Way out here . . . ?" I realized I had nodded into the phone. "How long?" the voice from below added, dreamy and reckless.

I turned to ask O'Hara and stared into the empty twilight of the wheelhouse and the emptier darkness of the wings.

"I don't know. . . ."

I had repeated it before I was aware the connection was gone.

18

THE FOLLOWING NIGHT, it was, I awoke instantaneously to what I had unconsciously been expecting. All the lights had gone out. The ship, with no way on, hung as tacit as a rundown clock. Her masts like giant hands did not stir among the stars. With the terrible softness and everlasting hush of a jungle island she lay in her own deep shadows and black heat. The darkness and stillness of death had crept evilly on her while I slept. She might as well have been fathoms down in the murky sea, and I drowned upon her decks.

In the early hours of the second morning I heard noises as if some kind of revel were being celebrated below — music so off-beat and off-key that it sounded authentically primitive, tuneless muffled song and muffled laughter. Hanging over the gunwale of my lifeboat to hear more distinctly I caught sight of two of the crew passing along the deck. The ray of a torch darting across their bearded faces produced an eerie effect as of prowling satyrs, and I experienced a keen, strange, suffocating thrill.

As the days and nights flowed on while nothing appeared to happen — though I felt something, perhaps everything, was happening — I lay remembering and wondering. What was O'Hara trying to prove? Why had he not taken over and conned us to our destination? Or was that too routine? Had he been afraid — not of mutiny so much as of what it would cost him to be repudiated and put down by his men? Had he in effect become one of them, not from fear and cowardice but from a nameless impulse toward community? Perhaps he had somehow, in a subtler way than any of the rest of us, himself succumbed. Something new, some untoward ambivalence had certainly come over him when the Old Man felled himself that night in the wheelhouse, an indefinable change, an elusive kind of negative realization which had seized him unaware and turned him upside down or inside out, the discovery perhaps of an opposite pole of himself. It was not a moment or a state of indecision because it seemed to me he had decided to recognize what had not been revealed to him before. There was in his action a touch, just a touch, of some kind of forbearance, as if he had taken unto himself the Old Man's heart-breaking corruption. He had issued an order. Was it rational? In whose name? In the captain's. But who was the captain? I mean at that instant. For afterward no one was. The ambiguity itself, left entirely to itself, apparently was paralytic or sterile.

I lived those ensuing days when sky and water were a unit of sunlit haze and the sun had no circumference, those nights traversed later and later by an inflamed moon, the way a lover dwells in morbid fantasies of nothing beyond every curve and crevice of a total infatuation which he never openly or actively indulges. I lived on my mattress in the shade of the lifeboat's tarpaulin as if eternally abandoned to a privacy of Dionysian fancies that destroyed thought and abhorred intrusion. And the rhythm of this life was unmarked except by an oceanic time, which I heard ticking intermittently far under me at the ship's keel and reverberating distantly but gigantically through her empty iron bowels.

When I had to have food I visited the galley on tiptoe, circumspectly in the dead of night, for then, since the ship had no lights, I ran the least chance of encountering any of the crew. Once, being surprised by one of my shipmates while filling my water cask at the spigot of the coffee urn, I trembled as though he had come to apprehend me. Staring blindly into the beam of his flashlight I felt annihilated, deprived of my very existence. I scarcely heard his exclamation or my own, but as my water cask crashed to the deck fled past him in the dark and flung myself into my lifeboat, where I hid sweating and panting like a man caught in the act of committing some heinous crime. I might have been stealing the last precious drops of water aboard for the sense of guilt I had.

On another occasion I ventured below in daylight to get a towel from my locker, since I swam continually in a profusion of sweat. With the ventilators becalmed the fiery radiation from the deck plates by day transformed the betweendeck spaces into a crematory smelling foully of human flesh. As I opened my locker the last letter I had received from home fell out at my feet. The sight of my mother's handwriting was all at once intolerable to me. I thrust the letter back under all my clothes as far as it would go, closed the locker and retreated to my lifeboat.

Lying there for the next few hours I could not divert my thoughts from that letter in my mother's writing, with my name neatly inscribed on the envelope — she wrote a conventionally clean legible hand — underneath my clothes at the far end of the locker. This became so tormenting an invasion of my world that I returned for the letter and without looking at what I was doing tore it by the rail into tiny shreds, which fluttered down and lay washing against the hull as they drank up the oily sea.

Throughout that period the shortest excursion I had to make from my sanctuary in the lifeboat had the magnitude of an expedition into a hostile wilderness. I undertook each one with pathological reluctance only after it could no longer be postponed, and dispatched it with almost frenzied haste and evasiveness so as to get back as soon as possible and without interruption to the purity of my solitude and the hypnotic torpor induced by that giant submarine ticking.

Only in the early stage was the almost comatose peace of my existence disturbed. One noon as I looked up into the gray canvas through which I could actually see the sun on the meridian as through a smoked glass, my reflections were broken by the inarticulate howls of a man having a nightmare or a child throwing a tantrum. They were joined by the shouting of one or two other voices, which sounded coherent though I could not distinguish their sense. There was the noise of a scuffle — grunted curses and thumping footsteps, growing louder and finally emerging onto the main deck.

The slightest sound was enough to trigger my pulses, and after the first rush of blood I lifted the loose edge of the tarpaulin where I climbed in and out of the boat, and witnessed beneath me two bearded figures wrestling and two more lurching around trying to interfere. They were all stripped to the waist, wearing zorris on their feet, and I would have found it impossible to recognize any of them had it not been for the pouting woman tattooed on one of the wrestlers and the fallen woman washing the feet of Jesus on the other.

Sayles's mouth was held agape emitting one weird ululation on top of another and resembling a deep head wound, while Costello, his gritted teeth gleaming through his black whiskers, gripped him struggling, one arm hugging his middle from behind and the other under his chin cocking his face skyward. Taking advantage of his weight Costello was slowly working him toward the rail, when with a sudden rush and recovery of his center of gravity he flung him clean and high over the side. With the protracted howl of a man falling into a chasm Sayles hit the ocean in an astounding splash, and the creamy water flowed over his head.

"What the hell ails him?" asked one of the bearded figures — I could no longer identify voices.

"Lover boy —" gasped Costello, leaning on his hands on the rail, his head hanging.

"Why'd he jump you — gone asiatic?"

Costello waggled his head. His fat back heaved as he sucked to recover his breath. "Poor son of a bitch —" he panted — "is in love!"

"Christ amighty —" the other croaked in amazement. To his companion he said, "Get a rope."

"He's better off where he is." Costello straightened and gazed tranquilly overboard at the slick of the Indian Ocean. "Let him drown. It's the only thing. He really needs to. The poor son of a bitch."

The other two idly joined him at the rail, and I was equally satisfied. I found myself accepting Costello's nihilism placidly, without qualm or question. Sayles, like the Bohunk and Sparks, had been absorbed into the sea and everything was peaceful. It was better that way.

But the radiant pluperfection of this truth was eclipsed the instant his black head punctured the surface. I felt distracted and harassed. His small weedy head was a presumptuous blot on the immaculate expanse of ocean.

He choked feebly and could not speak. His arms flopped unimportantly on the water. He made a gurgling noise that sounded like a cry for help.

"You sure you want to come aboard?" Costello spoke curiously, wonderingly to him, as to a castaway who had never seen the *Belle* before.

This time Sayles managed to ejaculate, distorted and bubbly, his claim on the others.

"It won't help." Costello shook his head. Then, incredulously, he startled me by adding, "Throw him the line."

The rope darted out and fell directly over Sayles. He clutched at it ludicrously, succeeded in tying it under his arms, and the three of them hauled him up the side like a fish. When they had him half over the rail they stopped hauling.

"Leave him hang there and dry out," said Costello. "The silly bastard."

His legs dangling outboard, head and arms inboard, water dribbling from his mouth and nose, they left him. By and by he gagged briefly, twitched himself over the rail and fell on the hot deck, where he lay quietly awhile in the sun before crawling away.

19

JUST ONCE was my privacy seriously threatened with
disclosure, yet this single narrow escape was so prolonged in its implications that I never afterward slept soundly
or woke rested. It occured, in the beginning, during the
quick interval of dusk. I had been roused from a doze by
footsteps coming along the boat deck. They came from forward aft. At first I thought they were made by a pair of
zorris, and that the peculiar double tread was the loose heels
clopping between feet and deck. But then the sounds were
so distinct I decided there must be two separate sets. They
were not ambling. They came slowly but directly, with mysterious purpose, toward my lifeboat, where they stopped.

I can't explain why I got it into my head that someone
had come to murder me, but I was so sure this was the errand that I felt inch by inch down the side of my mattress
to where, along with a flashlight, I kept my sheath-knife.
When I opened the strip that held the knife from falling
out of the sheath the snap was like a pistol shot. I eased
myself onto my haunches and held the knife ready at the
gunwale to disembowel whoever tried to climb over it into
my boat.

I seemed to hear breathing beneath me, but otherwise

there had been no noise for nearly three minutes since the footsteps had stopped. I could easily have heard the slightest whisper, so I assumed that whoever it was conversed by signals in the dusk, or had between them so hideously perfect an understanding that communication was unnecessary.

As I shifted my weight after a few moments to relieve the cramped muscles of my calves and thighs, the joint in my right knee cracked like another pistol shot. It must have been heard. I held my breath, listening for a movement outside. There was none. The wait was becoming unbearable. I did not dare indulge in the luxury of the least motion for fear another of my joints would crack.

I considered plunging between the tarpaulin and gunwale and flinging myself upon one of them from above. I would have the advantage of surprise and momentum. I could stab him on the way down and deal with the other afoot. But on the point of flexing myself I realized this was just what they would be expecting me to do. Why else would they be doing nothing but standing out there? I recovered myself in time to hear the clop of *zorris* proceeding away from me forward along the boat deck.

I tried openmouthed to catch further sounds, letting my breath in and out slowly. It must have been a delusion, but the air seemed to carry a thin, familiar scent. I cautiously raised the edge of the tarpaulin on the back of my hand and peered out. The dusk was thickening rapidly. I sought to penetrate it by staring obliquely first out of the tops, next the bottoms, next the corners of my eyes.

Finally I thought I could distinguish a shadowy figure standing by the forward lifeboat. He appeared to be doing something at the gunwale, probably unfastening the tarpaulin searching for me. So, I thought, he did not know exactly where I was. And then I realized that he was two fathoms tall!

With the shock of discovering I was being hunted down by a monster, the moment of shadowy discernment evanesced

144

in darkness and the abominable man, or whatever it was, dissolved in the middle of his antics into a thousand formless shades.

Several minutes passed before I was able to make myself explain the phenomenon. What I had no doubt seen was two persons, one of them boosting the other into the lifeboat. The first one inside would have hauled the second after, and this would account for the apparition's sudden vanishing.

This rational accounting gave me a short spell of relief until I was overtaken by the revelation that these men were planning to lie in wait in the other boat to spy me out. Far from searching for me, they must have known which boat I was in by the loose section of tarpaulin if nothing else. Their strategy put me at an impossible disadvantage. Sooner or later two of them could easily catch me, alone, by keeping watch in shifts. They had only to wait till I was obliged to leave my hideout and ambush me when I was returning. I lay despairingly back on my mattress and tried to decide what I should do.

There was absolutely no way I could really protect myself. The best tactics I could devise were to make all my excursions abroad in the dead of night, sneaking out and back circuitously, never climbing out or in at the same end or from the same side of the lifeboat, and taking what sleep I could get during the day. It was less likely though by no means impossible, especially once their patience had worn through, that they would attempt to jump me in daylight hours. It occurred to me, of course, that I might quit the lifeboat and return to my old berth below, but somehow this now seemed to be the worse even of such evils. Tempting as it was I also abandoned the idea of tricking them by locating myself in one of the port lifeboats. Since there were two of them and one of me, the temporary loss of surveillance all round was more disadvantageous to me than to them. I was safer staying where I could keep at least some track of their maneuvers.

In the morning when I peered out from under the tarp I noticed at once that the tarpaulin of the forward boat was fastened along the entire length of the gunwale. Since this would have been humanly impossible to do from inside, the occupants must have left the boat, or it could have been that one of them had left taking pains to lace the other in so that there would be no clue to his presence. They were certainly being very crafty and furtive in their actions. Try as I did I could not help the thought of the abominable thing recurring at intervals. But I managed fairly successfully to reject it. Whatever the advantage two ordinary human beings had over me, murderers though they might be, it was nothing to the other, and so I preferred to account for the phenomenon on the first grounds.

The only other possibility was that I had misinterpreted the dusky shadows of the evening before, and whoever it was had gone away without climbing into the boat. But compelling as this more conventional assumption was I could not take a chance on it. I could not afford to be tricked.

No one came topside all that day, and it was not till well after dark that I thought I heard again the traipsing of zorris on the deck. This time they did not come near me however, and sounded so faintly up ahead that I was not altogether sure my imagination was not playing with me. I thought I detected them several times, over a rather long period. I strained my eyes and made out nothing at all in the blackness; I strained my ears and caught no further noises. I lay struggling against sleep with my knife in my hand, and in the early silence before daybreak took it with me when I left the lifeboat.

Every night thereafter I heard the obscure clopping, and every day peeked out to find the tarpaulin of the forward lifeboat secured. For a while I hoped whoever it was would try to board my fastness so that I could seize them and stab them in the bowels. But from the very imagining of such primitive action I shrank in horror. I had next a desperate urge to force things to a showdown, to confront these stalkers of my privacy, hide on deck in the dark till the footsteps came, sneak upon the boat at midnight, or with my knife rip open the tarpaulin at midday. But any one of these moves, I thought, might be fatal.

And then gradually I built up an unchanging rhythm of defense against the unchanging rhythm of the danger. That is to say, I adapted myself to it as part of the whole impending matter.

20

SOON nothing penetrated my insulation. I drifted into a profound apathy. My lifeboat, threatened and vulnerable though it was, was apparently too good a fortress to be rashly stormed, and the rusting hulk on which it depended remained possessed by unseen presences that as yet had no more to do with me than ghosts and were no more nor any less real.

For a while there were the jarring notes of iron doors or hatches being clanged shut in various places about the ship, the occasional creaking and chafing of rigging whenever the hull rocked subtly and unreasonably as if gravity faltered, now and then the secretive murmur of voices below me, once or twice a night in the direction of the captain's cabin a hollow lonely lunatic cry raving out upon the silence.

In my lifeboat I was not disturbed and my consciousness was free to roam at will over the sequence of events which ended here. Or almost here, for though I could not have cared less at the time, I knew that this could not be quite the end, that while I was not in motion something else entirely unrelated was gigantically ticking away, that the final event unknown as it was had to be building up out of the malevolent heat, behind the malevolent masks of sunlight and darkness, like the corroding mechanism of a bomb set to go off at some unforseeable and indifferent hour. All the sense of future that I had was of this meaningless unwinding, while the present seeped into the past as easily as rainwater into a subterranean stream.

One night there was a particularly deathly quiet. The loose edge of the tarpaulin I had thrown daringly back hung from itself without a flutter. On my back gazing at the stars I saw them as scattered draughtless embers, coals burning cloudy red in the cosmic ashes, with now and then a meteor shooting from their center like a hot and short-lived spark. All at once, lying there lulled by my elaborate fancies and the long, remote, but exceptionally audible strokes resounding against the ship's bottom, I began to believe that this was not the ticking of a planetary clockwork at all but the knocking of an imprisoned spirit trying to get out of one of our holds, or doomed one trying to get in, or one of them trying to communicate with the other in some infernal code.

The impression took on me so strong a grip that I could not stay still. I picked up the electric lantern and my knife and climbed from the lifeboat. I tiptoed in bare feet along the boat deck till I found the ladder to the main deck. On the main deck I hesitated, while the plating, still not cool after the broiling day, heated the soles of my feet like warm lava. There was no sound whatever throughout the ship, and for a suspenseful second I thought even my ticking had ceased, or had perhaps never existed.

Then I heard its sepulchral clang. I waited intensely a minute till I heard it again. It was louder than it had been from the lifeboat and seemed to be located somewhere deep below and amidships. Not daring to show my light topside I groped my way artfully along the passageway. When I reached the door to the engine room I paused once more and listened.

The calmness and the peace of extinction were on the

entire ship. As I undogged the door and opened it — the pendulum swung, or the damned soul hammered at his alphabet, and the black limbo ahead of me rang dully and was immediately repossessed by a vast absorbing silence. The strokes I judged to be a minute apart, possibly with slight variations, and I held back through three of them, in an enthralling equilibrium where attraction was exactly balanced by repulsion, so that I could neither stay up or go down. But before the fourth stroke I had closed the door behind me without dogging it, and commenced my descent.

It was as if like a diver I was descending all the way to the bottom of the sea, which was the center of the earth. I had all the sensations of pressure, shallowness of breath, absence of spatial reference and of a sense of my own motion. The nerve signals between my ears and my brain lagged, so that with each new tick I started but not until long after it had rung. I was acutely apprehensive yet unable to reason why, and I worried about time as though my air supply were limited and might run out upon the passing of any one of these marked minutes.

Traversing the grating of the upper level I switched on my light to guide me, and recoiled. A swarm of winged shadows pursued me as I began descending to the second level. There indescribable shapes and shades moved elusively on the black surrounding air, following one another in a rout, merging, passing, changing, disappearing. I wondered whether perhaps my abominable man was among them.

Each stroke grew more pronounced as I descended the void that gaped beneath the open grating under my feet. On the third level the ship's engine rose above me, a three-headed monster with prostrate, distended, lumpish shadows all about it. The air was dank and foul, and I could hear the turbid wash and drip of water.

I was directly on top of the stroke now, and so close I thought I could actually feel its vibrations. I got down on my knees to probe the dark recesses with the shaft of light from my lantern, and disclosed, grinning up at me, the open jaws of a large Stillson wrench. It lay on its back in a crevice where it had fallen or been dropped, trapped in perfect balance by the structure of the hull, and with each imperceptible roll of the ship it canted over on invisible impulse and struck iron.

Here was my global pendulum!

I reached down, seized it, and rushed back up the ladders one forward of and above the other, across the gratings, the lantern swinging wildly in one hand, careless of the din of the wrench banging against rungs and rails. Arriving on deck breathless I flung without pausing the great wrench in a brief black arc overboard into the sea. . . .

I spent the next morning going over the incident as you do a dream, and I might never have persuaded myself that it was not a dream except for the total stillness. My ticking had stopped, which would certainly prove — or so I supposed — that I had indeed gone below in the night, found a wrench, a Stillson wrench, come up on deck and thrown it over the side. Yet if the ticking had not been real to begin with I had left myself no tangible evidence of anything. I forced myself to regard the whole adventure as having taken place in fact, but if in fact it did, it so divided me that I have ever since had to assimilate it as you would an act of somnambulism.

It was not merely from immortal longings that I had thrown time overboard irrecoverably into the unsounded depths of the Indian Ocean; it was, or so it seemed to me now, also a revolt against passivity. It was not much of a revolt; it was really a little act, not much more in fact than a gesture, but enough more to represent impatience with inaction, an assertion of self however inconsequential. Its significance was, practically speaking, negligible, but morally speaking perhaps tremendous in that any action — right, wrong, or merely foolish — has a vitality lacking in inaction. In other words, as I subsequently viewed it, there comes a time when waiting it out is morally impossible, when doing anything at all is better than doing nothing, when a sin of commission is preferable to a virtue of omission, when wisdom is more than — if I may be excused the expression — a finger up the ass and a mind in neutral. I say there comes a time. What you have to do is know when it is. Otherwise what you do is merely from lack of endurance.

The days that followed were an unblemished waste, while the humid, frightful calm shimmered on my sight, trembled in my nerves, made my stomach queasy, my heart palpitate, my head churn, till everything was dissolving — everything except the one last-straw-like realization to which I clung because I knew there was then nothing else. I must by my teeth, by my nails, by the single remaining tendon of my consciousness hang on — hang on — hang on. . . .

I lived through that dissolution and I survived, though not intact — possibly because I was too intact. What I mean to say is: I barely saved myself.

21

ALL TOLD, infected by the concupiscent heat, our light-less vessel, as dark by day as by night, with her chronom-eters unwound, lay festering in those scummy, tumescent seas twenty-three days, until the twenty-fourth of August, when she was hailed by a United States destroyer. The sound of an immense voice from the destroyer's bull horn two hundred yards off detonated the primordial silence like a clap of ghastly thunder.

"Ahoy, the Liberty — ahoy, the Liberty!"

Minutes passed, while nothing happened and I lay in my lifeboat rigid with the ugly shock of exposure.

"Aboard the Liberty — are you in trouble?"

The disciplined voice, amplified and superhuman, came as though out of a whirlwind.

Presently I caught the noises of activity at a distance, small distant cries of men, then the drone of a small engine being started. For a second I was swept by frenzy. They were sending a boat!

The motor noise grew louder. I crawled to the outboard gunwale of my life boat and lifted the edge of the tarpaulin which had sheltered me. The destroyer was hove to, thin, black, and sinister with the rising sun behind her. Her whaleboat was rounding in to our side directly below me, so that I looked straight down upon the covered heads of its occupants. Besides the coxswain and the engineer there were an officer, a petty officer, and two seamen, all wearing sidearms.

"Aboard there —" shouted the officer. "Give us a ladder!"

They waited a while with flower-like upturned faces, and the whaleboat knocked gently against our rusty plates.

"Break out the boarding ladder," ordered the officer. I could see the single bars on his clean shirt collar flashing in the sun. He was tall and young, a lieutenant junior-grade. The two seamen got the ladder hooked over our rail, tested it with their weight, then they climbed aboard us, the lieutenant junior-grade first, the petty officer next, and finally the seamen.

Underneath me the officer said, "Something's wrong all right."

"Damn queer," the petty officer agreed. "Don't seem like there's nobody aboard."

"Stand by here with Gibbs," the officer said with brusque authority to the petty officer. "Scarborough and I will have a look around."

When they had gone the petty officer said, "I hope this detail don't hold us up. I need that liberty in Sydney so bad I can taste it."

"Go below and open the seacocks on the old tub," the other suggested. "She wouldn't be no loss to nobody."

"If she's been abandoned," the petty officer observed, "she's like as not about to sink of her own accord."

"Then our lieutenant is in command and he can go down with her," said the seaman gaily.

The few minutes that they conversed below were for me ones of perfectly detached omniscience. My privacy had culminated now in an exhilarating delusion of invisibility in which, disembodied as the purest spirit, undetected and untouched, I could oversee human events with the wisdom of the ages and clairvoyance equal to the gods'. How ridicu-

154

lously limited was the vision of these paltry men! How silly, how duped, how fumbling they were! I knew all — they knew nothing. I saw and heard them; they did not even suspect my existence, let alone my prescience. I viewed past, present, and future in one transcendent illumination. Relieved of all earthly ties I stood free in the very center of truth and embraced its whole essence. I knew precisely what was going to happen in their lives in the next few minutes, while they — they had not the slightest inkling! They had no more perception than blind men. I would not for my life have let them in on it. It was too good. They were not worth it. They were children in their innocence and ignorance, living in a world of play — of games like pin-the-tail-on-the-donkey.

My body began to shake with soundless uproarious laughter in my expectancy of their awakening when the blindfolds came off and they saw revealed in one dazzling incredible flash what I had seen all along.

"Hey, Gibbs!" shouted one of the men in the whaleboat. "What is it — a floating whorehouse?"

"If it is," Gibbs replied in a lower tone, "stand by to pick up our lieutenant when he jumps over the side."

The men in the boat guffawed. One said, "What's he doing all this time — playing post office?"

"Knock off that talk," the petty officer said heavily, "our lieutenant comes of a good background."

He had hardly got out the remark when the lieutenant junior-grade was there at the rail by the boarding ladder, facing away from the ship in the direction of the destroyer.

"My God. . . !" he said, speaking out across the whole Indian Ocean.

"What's below, sir?" asked the petty officer.

"Stand by as you are on deck. Gibbs and Scarborough, you stand by with him." The lieutenant junior-grade cut off the petty officer behind. "I'm taking the whaleboat over to the ship to speak to the captain."

He swung a leg over the rail and climbed down the ladder. His sunburnt wholesome face was taut. He seemed deliberately to avoid looking at his men, as if he could not bear the sight of anyone.

"Get the Liberty's ladder over," he called back as the whaleboat pulled away.

Watching the whaleboat cover the distance to the destroyer, lying malignly official against the morning sun, I felt my laughter give way to emptiness and nausea. It had come to me that when the blindfolds did come off I was part of what the boarding party was going to find. The center of truth would be shifted and my exquisite privacy, my invisibility, my godly perception, my very existence — all would be destroyed by one methodical survey.

Then the game would go into another round, only this time I would be drawn into it as one of the blindfolded. . . .

22

IT MUST have been upwards of a half-hour before men began to gather on the deck of the destroyer. Meanwhile the three left aboard the *Belle* were struggling and cursing trying to rig her accommodation ladder. In spite of the clashing of iron which rang raucously through the ship, no one came on deck that I could see. Was there life within still, or were my shipmates all dead and the *Belle* a morgue? What exactly had the lieutenant junior-grade found to sicken and astound him? My foreknowledge was not so complete as I had fancied.

One after the other the destroyer's men went over her side into the waiting whaleboat. When the whaleboat was loaded to the rails, so that with its reduced freeboard and double ends it resembled a big gray war canoe, it backed away, swung slowly toward the *Belle*, and began to close the brazen space between.

The men below me at last got the accommodation ladder in place, and as the laden whaleboat settled against it I once more had the impression of gazing down upon the upturned faces of flowers. Most of the men — there must have been at least twenty-five — wore blue denims with white hats nodding like daisies in a breeze. While four in the stern sheets, the officers, were in khaki. All were as polished as brightwork on a yacht. They came aboard the *Belle* in formal order wearing sidearms, the lieutenant junior-grade, followed by another lieutenant junior-grade wearing medical corps insignia, and two ensigns, the first lean, small and sharp-faced, the second as bulbous as a Portuguese man-o'-war and as brilliant of countenance. Then the enlisted men filed up the ladder. In spite of differences in age they all looked simply young. They were mere boys.

The lieutenant junior-grade who had first boarded the *Belle* began issuing orders to his petty officers to search the ship. His flat, strong voice, confident in its clichés, was even from a distance unpleasant to hear.

"I want every man who can stand on his feet — if he has to be helped help him — mustered aft on the main deck," he announced. "Doctor," he went on, modifying his tone, "before you attend to the captain you can arrange to have the corpsmen set up sickbay in the ship's hospital and the officers' mess. Give me a report as soon as you can on the condition of the worst ones. Mr. Twombley," he addressed the fat beaming ensign in his former peremptory voice, "I want identification of all members of ship's company and their records."

"Aye, sir," Twombley snapped, saluting with a great jiggle of waist. The doctor, without saluting, had walked casually off.

"Mac —" the lieutenant called, "where are you going?"

"Below to see what she's got left for guts," said the sharp-faced ensign, and departed unceremoniously, squinting as though the sunlight bothered him.

"Let me know —" the lieutenant junior-grade called belatedly, and stopped. "Guns —" He turned to a tall stooped petty officer. "Round up any small arms."

Inevitably the *Belle's* crew began to appear in twos and

threes, blinking, shielding their eyes with their hands or lowering their heads in the ruthless sun, escorted by the destroyer's men. Bearded, disheveled, unkempt, soiled — they were unrecognizable most of them from where I was. White corneal glances flickered from grizzled heads as they shambled erratically across the deck and collected dazedly in a growing cluster where they were pushed stumbling, looking confused and withdrawn like prisoners who have been rotting in a dungeon or madmen emerging from asylum. They had lost either the desire or the power to speak. Now and then one would be supported on deck apparently drunk or sick, his feet wandering, his arms over the shoulder of one of his mates or a sailor. They were as uniform in their dishevelment as the navy men were in their spanking clean blue denims and white hats. Five of the latter rode herd on the group while the lieutenant junior-grade kept an eye on things from an executive distance.

I was engrossed in these proceedings without any thought that I was myself or would shortly become a part of them, when I found myself staring full into the alerted eyes of a sailor whose face had just appeared above the after edge of the boat deck a few feet away. Only then I realized that in the keenness of my concern I had thrust my head and neck clear out from under the tarpaulin, clear out over the gunwale of my lifeboat, in plain sight of anyone who might happen to glance my way. With the instinct of a turtle or a snail I started to draw in. But there was no use. I had no shell to protect me — nothing at all except a frail, useless fabric. I was caught out at last and would have to stay out.

But unable any longer to withdraw I was equally unable to advance. I simply hung limp over the gunwale of the lifeboat. The sailor cleared the top of the ladder, stepped to one side, and, as I saw at the level of his feet another white hat rising above the edge of the boat deck, to my innocent astonishment snatched his sidearm from its holster and aimed it directly into my eyes.

Gaining the deck the second sailor observed the automatic at the end of his companion's extended arm and followed its aim to me. Thus I had my first close look in some weeks at clean-shaven faces. They seemed foolishly bare and resolute, at the same time touched with uncertainty and suspicion that for the moment I found quite incomprehensible. No one could have felt more vulnerable and less menacing at that point than I did.

"What is it?" asked the second sailor. His pronoun made me feel like a freak, as though I belonged to no recognizable species. "A stowaway?"

All at once for the first time in a long while I was filled with the need to speak, where only minutes before I would have gone to any lengths to protect myself against doing so. The urgency came overpoweringly upon me.

"I belong to the ship's company." The voice simply did not sound like my silent voice to which I had been listening for so long. I heard the words, but realized at once that I hardly believed what they said. I scrutinized the two sailors to see if they sensed anything false.

"Okay, you," the first sailor said, gesturing with the automatic. "Come out of it." Again the pronoun fell unpleasantly on my ear. "Hit the deck."

Not even then was I aware that I looked to them no different from the rest of the crew being assembled on the main deck. Whatever made me suppose I had been immune to the same cumulative untidiness, the same degeneration of appearance, I will never know. I was still puzzled by their guarded and hostile tone.

"I'll see he gets below, and be back. You go ahead with the other boats," the first sailor said to the other man when I reached the deck.

His instructions recalled to me my intangible neighbors. I glanced at the forward boat long enough to ascertain that its tarpaulin was laced down. Now that danger had defined itself in concrete form they seemed to be sheer hallucination.

"You don't need to hold that gun on me," I protested, raising my strange voice.

"Down the ladder, buddy," the sailor said. It was a curious designation, curiously pronounced. I had heard it before.

When I joined the group of my shipmates only two or three briefly glanced up askance at me. Most of them were beyond interest. Therefore I had no insight into them. Without curiosity they revealed nothing of themselves, gave me nothing. They were inattentive. They seemed ready to allow any subjection of their initiative, any despotism, to be in fact gratified at being herded about like so many scraggly cattle. I was baffled and disconcerted to see no sign in them of recognition, and though at closer range I began to recognize them one by one, I felt a kind of foreignness about them all.

As I had passed the lieutenant junior-grade the sailor with me had said, "Found this stowed away in one of the lifeboats, sir." The lieutenant junior-grade had let his eyes rest on me without altering the frigid expression of authoritative distaste with which he viewed the entire scene. Nevertheless, I thought, he was enjoying himself.

Most foreign of all, though I had no difficulty after one glance in identifying him, was the steward when he came out and along the deck unescorted. For a second I had taken him to be one of the boarding party. He had no beard, his black oily hair was slicked down on his narrow skull, his dingy complexion seemed almost to glow with cleanliness. In spite of the heat he was in uniform — a freshly laundered, unwrinkled uniform in which he had obviously not yet even sat down. A khaki shirt with long sleeves, rolled down what was more, unusual and outlandish in that climate, hid his execrable tattoo, while under his arms the shadowy stains of an unaccustomed sweat were just beginning to show.

Lightly, deferentially, on tiptoe as if he did not wish to disturb anybody or call attention to his conspicuous self, he crossed over and halted a few respectful paces from the lieutenant junior-grade, his muddy eyes averted, appearing to

161

notice nothing while he took in everything. His tongue darted out and over his sallow lips. His stance was as near to attention as he had ever stood. It might have been a travesty of military decorum except that it somehow had the authority of perfect presence. Its poise said clearly that the steward at the moment was free from all attachment, ready to yield to the earliest and strongest necessity. I felt rather than observed the men around me stir slightly, in unison, as though afflicted together with a subtle spasm.

The lieutenant junior-grade went over the steward silently with the minute, corrective eye of the inspecting officer. It was obvious that the steward was making an impression. Like a somewhat tarnished piece of old brightwork he seemed to glow with unpretentious virtuosity.

"Name?" asked the lieutenant junior-grade.

"Armitt, sir. Ship's steward."

The lieutenant junior-grade started to say something and checked himself. He waved his left arm to the rear, away from the rest of us, and said, "Stand by."

The steward moved, or was wafted, behind the lieutenant junior-grade and took his special station by the bulwark with downcast gaze. It was impossible to determine precisely what his attitude reflected. It was faultlessly equivocal. It had the concentrated balance of an acrobat.

When about three quarters of our ship's company had been brought on deck the rolypoly ensign appeared with a paper in his hand.

"This is all of 'em able to stand muster," he told the lieutenant junior-grade. "We made up this roster here. It isn't alphabetical," he apologized.

"Not alphabetical!" the lieutenant junior-grade said censoriously.

"Not entirely — we didn't take the time," the ensign explained, showing confusion, and when the other stared thoughtfully in our direction, he too turned and examined us. "God," he said, "what a bunch of bums!"

"That will do," the lieutenant junior-grade told him. Stepping forward and confronting our incurious little community of disorder he raised his voice. "Now hear this — when your name is called step out and form a line 'thwartship starting from the port rail."

He nodded to the fat ensign, who began hallooing names from the sheet of paper which he held high and in front of his face with both hands. His pudgy cheeks were soaking wet. He might have been calling numbers in a Beano game for all the distinction made by his tone. Each name, formally exorcised of any personal or familiar quality, was sung out as though it were an accusation of the same offense.

When it happened that no one stepped forward in response the ensign called the name again, more accusingly, and after an unvarying interval, seeing from behind his paper that no one joined the line to his right, he called the next name on the list, which he momentarily laid on his broad flat thigh in order to mark the absence with a pencil. Frequently, as if they had not recognized their own names, men would suddenly start forward in company with the men whose names followed theirs. In such instances the ensign would repeat both names and impassively return the paper to his thigh in order to scratch off the absence mark. In spite of his impassivity each break in the rhythm of the muster seemed somehow portentous.

One after another and occasionally in confused pairs the men shuffled or hobbled wordlessly forth, and the embarrassed line grew crookedly to midships, while those of us not yet summoned out of anonymity regarded our shipmates' slouched, unseemly backsides.

The doctor came through the door and said to the lieutenant junior-grade, "We located it. Somebody aboard knows what he's doing. It's pretty professional." They conferred together as the muster proceeded.

The five guards ranged along the rear of the line.

"— Bo-*hoo*-nicky," enunciated the ensign. He made his

usual pause. "Aitch Bo-*hoo*-nicky —" After the second routine pause he laid the muster sheet against his thigh and marked the Bohunk absent.

The doctor left the lieutenant junior-grade and went up to the beginning of the line. He was young and tall, with stiff aristocratic features and a supercilious, untemperamental manner. His movements were swift and unhurried, beautifully schooled and callously economical. He pushed each man's left eyelid back with his right thumb exposing the eyeball, dropped his thumb to the lower lid pushing it down, simultaneously raised the right arm by the wrist in his left hand twisting the inside uppermost, dropped his right hand to raise the left arm by its wrist, glanced triangularly from left eye to right arm to left arm, dropping the right arm then the left, and took three steps to confront the next body. He moved along the line in an unbroken continuity of motion. Now and then as he dropped a left arm and took his three steps he would say in an undertone without looking at the man "Step forward," and the man would obey, head hung. He was mechanical, bored, resigned, as if he had no business being in the middle of the Indian Ocean and was there only because of the wasteful folly of mankind, against which precious medical skill had neither remedy nor defense.

He left in his wake two ranks, the advance one of drooping, widely separated, painfully isolated figures, the rear one denser but with here and there vacant places which the men tended, shifting uncomfortably, to close. Before the last two men were called into line he caught up with the muster and waited hands on hips before the empty position next to be occupied, his head tilted upward, gazing off at space.

When the final name on the roster had been called, and the last man was in line, the chubby ensign let the muster sheet fall to his side in one hand and looked at the lieutenant junior-grade. The latter strode athwartship, very deliberately and purposefully eying both ranks, came halfway back and mounted the hatch cover, which had the effect of a low

164

platform of increasing his stature a few inches. He was unquestionably a petty tyrant, enslaving the *Belle's* company with his implicit moral advantage, from a position so obviously impeccable at the moment compared with theirs. Still, it was an assignment quite beyond his experience, and not easy. You had to admire him a little. He stood his ground before the unheard-of and unspeakable.

"All right, now —" he began in a loud, clear, youthfully unconditional tone. "We want to know the source."

The men might have been still waiting for him to speak for all the response he got. Just then Sayles came out on deck flanked by two sailors. He was an abject sight. Big tears gathered in his eyes and rolled viscidly out and into his beard, and he was shaking as with profound cold. The sailors guided him aft along the starboard bulwark. One of them put an arm across his chest, halting him near where the steward was standing.

"The sooner you tell us the easier it will go with you," the lieutenant junior-grade said threateningly, after noting the arrival of Sayles. He bent an uncompromising gaze on the lonely figures between him and the rear line. After a minute of silence he said, "We will find out sooner or later. Not one jack of you will get out of custody until we know." He consulted his watch. "Who is that?" he inquired of the ensign, indicating Sayles.

"He says he's the second mate, sir," one of the sailors called over.

"Where are the other officers, Mr. Twombley?" the lieutenant junior-grade asked.

"The assistant engineers are in sickbay," the ensign explained hurriedly. "Mac is bringing the engineering officer. The third mate is intoxicated at the moment. I put a guard on him in his stateroom. The captain you know about. We found the chief mate on the flying bridge. I left a guard."

The lieutenant junior-grade scowled. "Why hasn't he been brought down here?"

The ensign hesitated. "He refused to come."

"He what!" the lieutenant junior-grade exclaimed, startled. "He refuses —"

"That is correct, sir. He said he will expect you up there."

"Expect me —" The lieutenant junior-grade was aghast. "He expects —"

Having anticipated facing no more complex problem than demoralization, which at worst might mean a sickly mutiny, the lieutenant junior-grade had assumed that he alone held title to protocol aboard. Unmoved by a man or by men, he was put off in plain sight by this rival in kind of the source of his security. He at once reinforced himself by asserting the superiority of his prerogative.

"Get him down here on the double. Arrest him if you have to. Take some men." He clamped his mouth shut and squared his shoulders.

"Aye, aye —" said the ensign and trotted ponderously off.

There was barely detectable general movement among the mustered men, as if they were surprised to discover that there could be anyone of the *Belle's* company who thought he had any privileges or rights left, let alone the audacity to insist on their not being summarily discounted. They must have entirely forgotten O'Hara.

It was at this point that Costello emerged, bare to the waist and barelegged, following the wiry sharp-featured little ensign whom he overwhelmed even from behind by the mere grossness of his neglected flesh. His white-skinned, black-haired paunch rolling over the top of his beltless trunks, he advanced like a majestic Silenus in the tow of a wry sprite.

The ensign, a dour Scot as gray and tough as a nail, came to a halt before the lieutenant junior-grade with a sardonic expression in his squinting eyes and on his thin lips. "This is the chief," he said. "Name's Costello."

The lieutenant junior-grade frowned maturely upon them both.

166

"Costello — are you prepared to lend my engineers a hand if they need it?" he asked austerely.

Costello emitted a nasty laugh. "They'll need it," he said. His normally clear tenor sounded as though it were clotted with sleep. He looked down with magnificent displeasure on the ensign. "Him and his fifty-thousand horses! Let's see him get a day's run out of my lousy twenty-five hundred!"

"I am asking you, Costello —" The lieutenant junior-grade scowled in meticulous, intransigeant authority. "Are you prepared to co-operate?"

"I'm a passenger," Costello replied in his throat. "He knows where I live. He'll be around."

The ensign said tersely, humorously, "You think."

"Lay up to your room," the lieutenant junior-grade ordered Costello. "You are confined to quarters." Costello spat on the deck. "And there will be no more of that sort of thing on this ship," the lieutenant junior-grade said, his face flushing. As Costello strode gluteally off, the other said to the ensign, "Mr. MacFarland, what about it?"

Ensign MacFarland, turning to leave, shrugged side-to his superior and kept going. "She's some clunker," he replied, not troubling even to talk over his shoulder. "It'll take time. It's a black hole of heat down there," he added indifferently.

His own bloodless complexion, slight build, and low metabolic rate promised immunity from the sweat that poured through the brows and into the eyes of ordinary engineers. Only a single drop of water, twinkling like a pearl, hung beneath the sharp point of his nose. He seemed born to live below deck, and no doubt it would be a minimum of assistance he would need from Costello, if he needed any.

"Put a guard on that chief engineer," the lieutenant junior-grade said. And when Ensign MacFarland did not reply, he called out, "Mr. MacFarland!"

Without turning his head or slacking his pace MacFarland said, "I need all my men."

The brotherhood of engineers, it appeared, was stronger

167

than the chain of command even in the navy. It was clear that Costello, hostile though he was, would have to be contained by someone other than Ensign MacFarland.

The lieutenant junior-grade stared hard but briefly at the retreating back of his engineering officer. Then he looked at his watch, lifted his chin, and raised his voice. "Now hear this, all of you —" At that instant he was interrupted by a sailor rushing on deck and up in front of him.

"Lieutenant — sir! Excuse me —" The sailor was the one who had held the gun on me. He spoke, sweating furiously as a result of his haste, in the great agitation of emergency.

"Well —" cut in the lieutenant junior-grade, giving the man his paternal frown. The sailor lowered his voice as if imparting information of confidential or obscene nature, which the lieutenant junior-grade took in with stony composure. However, the sun was beginning to cause the skin of his forehead and cheeks to weep.

"Where?" he asked sharply once.

The sailor gesticulated mysteriously with his arm. Finally he stopped talking and the lieutenant junior-grade studied his face as though he were searching it for some missing data. Suddenly he called out, "Doctor!" And when the doctor, who had been leaning elegantly against the bulwark, merely glanced up he added, "Will you step over here?"

For several minutes the three of them conferred too quietly to be heard. The lieutenant junior-grade addressed the doctor, the doctor addressed the sailor, and the sailor addressed the lieutenant junior-grade. At the sound of a heavy thud all three glanced around. One of the *Belle*'s crew, overcome by having to stand so long in the sun, had collapsed in his tracks on the burning deck.

The doctor detached himself and went over to the unconscious man. The lieutenant junior-grade told the sailor to stand by. Then he shouted, "Steward!"

The steward jumped like one who had been stung. He collected himself and started tiptoeing tentatively across the deck as if it were so hot that it burned through the soles of his shoes and seared his feet. Gliding smokily past the broken ranks of his shipmates he seemed to appeal to each one individually with damp oblique gaze.

As he halted, darting his tongue over his lips, a cry quavered on the air.

"No — no! Not him! He ain't the one! He ain't the one to blame —"

The unsteady cry was both frantic and beseeching. It had come from Sayles. For the moment he had stopped shaking and was standing wide-mouthed as though he were dazed by the sound of his own voice. Before his astonished escorts could make a move he darted forward. Running and hopping he made his way to the coaming of the hatch atop which the lieutenant junior-grade solemnly stood, mystified by this interruption.

"It ain't him, lieutenant," Sayles cried out in a whine of weird intensity. "I swear it ain't him!" For a second he appeared about to go down on his knees at the edge of the platform. He was prevented by his escorts running up and taking station on either side of him, as they watched the lieutenant junior-grade for a sign.

"What is it you're trying to say?" the lieutenant junior-grade asked distastefully.

"He ain't the one t' blame —"

"He's not being blamed for anything," replied the lieutenant junior-grade, in irritated disbelief at Sayles's queer behavior. "It's perfectly obvious to me he's the only one among you that has held onto himself."

As if he had not heard him Sayles wailed again, "It ain't him — I swear it! He ain't the one!"

The lieutenant junior-grade gave a perfunctory nod to the sailors, who seized Sayles's arms and began to drag him away. Unstruggling, commencing to shake once more, his feet stumbling on themselves, he put all his remaining energy into crying out, "I swear it — I swear it!"

"Pipe down, you!" ordered one of his guards, giving him a sharp wrench of the arm.

The doctor approached the hatch, and the lieutenant junior-grade said, "Steward! I'm assigning you to the doctor. You will take your orders from him."

After a noticeable pause the steward spoke a barely audible "Yes, sir."

Dispatching him on an errand, the doctor returned to the prostrate man, and the steward disappeared to port just as O'Hara came on deck to starboard.

With Ensign Twombley, ahead of two sailors, wading sweatily in his wake, O'Hara came aft walking strictly, his eyes straight ahead, and abruptly took a position in front of and back to the lieutenant junior-grade. He had on his uniform and cap, and the silver oak leaves on the collar of his shirt glittered fantastically. He put his feet down in his solid way, and as I noted his black gleaming shoes I thought once more of Bohunicky. The hectic rash glowed brightly on his face, neck, and arms, now washed clean of calomine. He was close-shaven, and the flesh of his cheeks, particularly under his eyes, looked bloated. He seemed to have noticed nobody.

There had arrived simultaneously that tension of attitude in everyone which was invariably a part of O'Hara's presence. Even the sick and wilted braced themselves. He alerted and invaded the very senses, for cutting through the familiar aromatic reek of bodies came the clean keen mordant smell of that inexplicable carbolic acid.

He spoke immediately, before anyone else could have a chance to, in a deadened monotone which nevertheless revived a shuffling, discomfited kind of life along the sad and squalid ranks of the *Belle's* company.

"I know the cause of this —"

Looking enigmatically ahead, he addressed himself like a communicant, not to the officer behind him nor to the men in front, but to something more general, to something mysteriously at large, to that mystical entity known as "the ship."

170

"I will take over this vessel and bring her to her proper destination."

This dutiful, ritualistic speech was, far from its superficial appearance of being a last assertion of status, the culmination of an obsession. It was late, but it was singular.

O'Hara was answered unexpectedly by a yell, and I glanced to starboard in time to see Sayles break the grasp of his escorts and come at a stumbling lope across the deck to accost O'Hara. He brandished both his trembling fists in O'Hara's face and screeched, "Yew are the one! It's yew to blame. . . !"

Like a dying man O'Hara seemed to observe nothing and nobody around him, not Sayles's fists before his unblinking eyes. Sayles, peaked, twitching, righteous from his citizenship in the equality of degradation, swelled to what he took for O'Hara's self-righteous superiority.

"Yew did it to us. . . . yew should have stopped it — yew could have stopped it. It's yew — yew — yew. . . !"

He shrieked it before all mankind, before all those there-but-for-the-grace-of-God sinners, the nameless and faceless men and women whose pride of frailty makes them scorn the strong, before the unresistant masses of the loving and lovable who find succor and power in the democracy of the fallen, before the undespised malefactors who eke out faith through deficiency and salvation through wrongdoing. He shrieked it over and over, this ineffectual second who had himself been often loved for fecklessness. He fairly danced like a witch doctor before his victim.

"They've got yore dirty ass now," he sneered hysterically.

Before the man who had never asked for nor received it, all his promiscuous compassion became perverted to wanton venom. He became senseless.

"Mister O'Har-ass —" He began to laugh rhetorically, thrusting his demented face up to O'Hara's. "Ha-ha-ha-ha-ha. . . ."

O'Hara appeared neither to see nor hear him.

"He-ho-har-ass!" he gibbered cunningly.

The lieutenant coming out of his astonishment swung his arm in a repelling arc. "Take this man away!" he commanded in a tone crackling with outrage.

Sayles's guards grappled him roughly between them. But there was no need. This little moment too of blind assault had passed. He wilted in their arms as if horrified by himself, and in the moaning voice of a mendicant begged everyone to exonerate and forgive the *Belle's* crew. He was half carried off and out of view, sobbing, sordid, mortifying in his insulting fidelity to weakness and his infatuation with suffering.

In this weakness and suffering he had always looked disparagingly enough on O'Hara as a mainstay, on the devious assumption that being tough he suffered less or not at all. Now, even more deviously, he had clung to him as a scapegoat. But the truly devious thing was suggested by the speculation that a man like O'Hara suffered most, that his capacity for this too was stronger and was preyed upon (and perhaps especially and suddenly in his case) by his capacity to be responsible for others, and by the merciless competition not of his equals but of the little men who were incontestably his inferiors. At that moment it seemed to me almost vicious that the aggrieved community of the pitiable should be so much more than a match for their grievously solitary betters.

Monosyllabically terse, the muscles of his healthy cheeks tightened, the lieutenant junior-grade had just said to the ensign, "Name!" indicating O'Hara's back by a spasmodic inclination of his head.

The ensign snatched his sheet of paper, which he had folded four times, from the wet breast pocket of his shirt, and ran a rapid eye over it. "O'Hara," he said. "K. O'Hara. Chief mate."

The lieutenant junior-grade made an official hacking sound to clear his throat, like a judge about to pronounce sentence. "O'Hara," he said with the omnipotent neutrality of a mere

172

instrument, "my assignment is to take what steps are required to bring this ship into Sydney under escort of the destroyer. For that operation I am in command here." His disciplined tone carried a freezing impersonality. "You will take orders from me — or from my duly authorized representatives."

In that second O'Hara had his chance at the luxury, the refuge of acquiescence. All the world loves a confessed sinner. Obviously whatever chance he had with the world now was only on the world's terms. He could even plead the world's morality in his own cause, explaining his refusal to take charge of the *Belle* as being the result of remorse for having wished the Old Man out of the way, which no doubt he had done many times over. The pronouncement of the lieutenant junior-grade was as much an offer as a threat. O'Hara could creep softly into the great warm womb of culpability, cover himself with the guilt of being born human, or he could stand erect coldly in the open and make the world confront him with it.

His posture was ambivalent. It was impossible to tell whether he assumed his stance intentionally to reduce the lieutenant junior-grade to the choice he could not afford to be pushed into of descending from the hatch or talking to his back, or whether by some late and latent instinct he had compulsively interposed himself for a single dedicated instant between his men and the unavoidable reckoning.

It was clear he asked nothing of them — they were too far gone in abject docility to support or deny him if they wanted to. His attitude was rather one of personal commitment so inward and intense as to be sacerdotal, in which very likely the men and the lieutenant junior-grade hardly figured at all. His fixed expression and immobility had the quality of pure abstraction, in their ignorance of which the neat young officer behind and the ragged ranks before shrank to insignificance.

The ear became aware of a random murmur — it was not

definable, not of sympathy or antagonism or wonder — it was the incoherent, troubled, passing sound of disturbed sleepers. The issue had been drawn — inescapable and intolerable. There was no real telling what he would do. For the one unknowable second of response allotted to him O'Hara did finally command the ship.

"I'll be damned first . . . !"

The supreme, the sublime conceit had asserted itself. The scorching whisper could have been heard by every man on the after deck, condemning and condemned. But though it was uttered to all space, it could not have been heard across the seas, or aboard the patrolling destroyer, or from the *Belle's* deserted open bridge, or in her closed spaces where the problems of recovery were beginning to be solved. It would never be entered in her official log. However vast and eternal its repercussions, it had been uttered out of spiritual darkness by a single man and was gone.

Of that ephemeral knot of men on the after deck who were able to hear, a few might have understood that this man's damnation was willed, and consisted of the fact that he was the only one who could, if he had wanted to, have prevented the fatal bargain, and did not purely because he would not. These few, who knew he was good for it, may also perhaps have assumed a share of culpability for this.

But not the lieutenant junior-grade. With a protestant gesture of dismissal he said promptly to Ensign Twombley, "Place this man under arrest. Lock him in his quarters and post a guard."

"Aye!" said the ensign, bouncing in his tracks and hastily stuffing the muster sheet which he had forgotten into his shirt pocket. He and the two sailors went to O'Hara, but once there they were at a loss what to do. They acted as though under an inexplicit constraint. They seemed to be incapable of laying a hand on him. The sailors looked at Ensign Twombley and Ensign Twombley wiped his palms up and down on his round hips.

174

Before the ensign and his sailors took him in custody O'Hara turned on his shining black heel and walked strictly back the way he had come. Awkwardly caught up with by his guards he passed from sight just as, by an odd symmetry of coincidence, the steward came gliding aft on the opposite side.

The lieutenant junior-grade summoned the doctor over and conversed with him and the sailor who had pointed his pistol at me. As these two were departing he called out, "Make sure the stowaway is safely confined under guard."

Safely confined under guard . . . I could have laughed aloud . . . the stowaway!

Then the lieutenant junior-grade glanced at his watch, lifted his chin, and the towering idiom boomed down on us once more.

"Now hear this —"

23

SHORTLY BEFORE sundown the engine-room telephone jangled in the pilothouse. The sunburned lieutenant junior-grade picked it up and snapped, "Bridge — Captain!" He no longer wore his sidearm, but there was a guard present carrying a Springfield. All about the ship hung the fresh, penetrating reek of oily soot.

On the other end of the phone was the destroyer's assistant engineering officer.

"Engine room reporting half manned and half ready." There was a pregnant pause and the voice added, "Captain, sir."

"Are you ready for sea?" inquired the lieutenant junior-grade primly.

There was another pause, after which the voice of Ensign MacFarland said, "Are you kidding, friend — ah, Captain? This teakettle is so primitive I had to spend most of the afternoon learning to forget what I was taught in school so I could figure out how to operate it."

The lieutenant junior-grade said, "Can you get under way?"

"You just give the word. Captain. We got about half a

load of steam on the old pot. We'll try to pick up the rest as we go along if you don't crowd us. Don't have your heart set on breaking any records. Can make maybe four, maybe five knots to start with."

"Four — is that even steerageway?"

"Search me. That's your department."

"Very well. Stand by," said the lieutenant junior-grade. "And belay the wisecracks."

"Aye, aye," said MacFarland, "— Captain."

The lieutenant junior-grade hung up. The rolypoly ensign came in, hatless, crew-cut.

"Are the passengers for the whaleboat ready?" the lieutenant junior-grade asked him briskly.

"Affirmative," said the ensign. "Both of 'em standing by. Doc's got the old man under sedation."

"Very well," said the lieutenant junior-grade. "Send the whaleboat back to the destroyer. We'll get under way in ten minutes. Report back."

"Aye, aye," replied the ensign jubilantly, and jounced down the passageway.

"Signalman —" the lieutenant junior-grade called.

"Signalman, aye," responded a sailor from the wing.

"Signal the destroyer. Under way in ten minutes, course one-eight-zero, speed four."

"Under way in ten minutes, course one-eight-zero, speed four. Aye, aye, sir!" repeated the sailor.

I listened to the rhythm of the shutter clicking smartly on the signal light, and read the answering flashes from the destroyer, which was now black in silhouette against the setting sun. The whaleboat, pulling away from us, came into view off our starboard bow. There was still light enough for me to see its passengers outlined in the stern sheets, one large and grotesquely shapeless as a scarecrow, the small one bright, stark, and implacable as a doll.

I underwent a humiliation that was not mine, not exactly mine, and said resentfully to the sunburned lieutenant junior-grade, "The least you might have done was send the Old Man over by himself!"

The lieutenant junior-grade laid his clear blue eyes on me, coldly speechless. Then he uttered his rebuke. "You are out of order." He presented his back to me. It was his position not ours that concerned him. The seriousness and actual fatuity with which he seized the duty of getting us back where we were not wanted or needed, and did not particularly desire to go, would have been asinine if it had not been so humiliating.

The signalman entered from the wing. "Message from the destroyer, sir. 'Course one-seven-four. Acknowledge.' "

"Very well," said the lieutenant junior-grade. "Acknowledge."

The signalman continued to read. " 'Initial speed four. Make best possible speed consistent with condition of machinery. Keep us informed.' "

The lieutenant junior-grade colored slightly under his sunburn. "Give them a wilco," he said.

"Aye, sir."

When the pudgy ensign Twombley returned, the lieutenant junior-grade asked, "What about the watches?"

"Well," said the ensign screwing up his round joyous face, "if we keep a guard it'll take all our men, but we got three of the others in fair enough shape to do duty as helmsmen." He chewed his nether lip. "The rest are in a hard way. The doc says some of 'em will probably have to be hospitalized in Sydney."

"Keep the guard," the lieutenant junior-grade ordered him. "What about the officers?"

The ensign rolled his eyes theatrically high up into his head. "The second's got a crying jag on — he's a mess. The young one I guess will be okay in a few hours once he's sobered off."

"When he's in shape use him," replied the lieutenant junior-grade. "But confine him to his quarters like the others

178

when he's off watch. Have the steward take them their meals. He can be counted on. This man here," he added, indicating me, "has his papers and can help out. I'll take the conn with him till you get squared away."

"Roger," said the ensign, with boundless enthusiasm.

"What about the prisoner?" This was now O'Hara's designation and his office.

"Locked in his stateroom."

"Very well. Stand by to get under way." The lieutenant junior-grade glanced at his watch. "Take the helm," he ordered me. He rang the engine-room telephone. "Bridge to engine room — stand by to answer all bells."

"*All* bells —" The engineer's voice came out loud and clear. "Now, ah, Captain — don't you get gay with this septic tank."

"Give me what you can and let me know when I can have more," the lieutenant junior-grade curtly amended. "Make turns for four knots."

"Turns for four — will try," replied the engineer. "Hang on to your hat — here we go!" And he added — "Captain."

Ensign Twombley went below and the lieutenant junior-grade stepped to the annunciator and rang up Slow Ahead. "Left full rudder," he said to me.

I spun the wheel to left full. The destroyer had her boat hoisted and now swung stern to off our port beam. Once again the *Liberty Belle* came to her bumbling life, took up her familiar thumpings and groanings, and was under way once again, winding soddenly to port, as though she had again, however lethargic or recalcitrant, a purpose.

"Course is one-seven-four," the lieutenant junior-grade instructed me.

I eased the helm ten degrees.

"Answer up!" he commanded.

"Course one-seven-four," I repeated obediently, wanting for a passing second to laugh both in bitterness and relief.

The organization had taken us up at last.

179

We were on course and had the destroyer dead ahead at approximately one thousand yards, lighting our way and laying our track with her wake, a meticulous custodian of our future, when the jolly ensign came crashing and stumbling along the passageway. He halted breathless before his superior, his eyes showing white all round their brown pupils.

"The chief mate — the redhead —" he sputtered, forgetting O'Hara's new formal status. "He's killed himself!"

The lieutenant junior-grade was absolutely stunned. For the first time, before the morally unexpected, he revealed insecurity in the unseeing movement of his head from side to side like a blinded animal. For all his elaborate precaution he had failed to stay on top of every possibility. This failure was a terrific shock to him, which a touch of Simms's skepticism might have mitigated. But the lieutenant junior-grade was no skeptic. I could see him blaming himself, like a dog who gets accidentally struck when he is not looking.

"My orders were to lock up all the firearms —" he began defensively, and bogged down. He was obviously thinking about having to report this unfavorable incident to his commanding officer.

"I did — I did. I locked 'em all up," the ensign protested devoutly. "He used a razor blade. He slashed his wrists with a razor blade and bled to death in his sack! I never thought a man could have so much blood —"

Both his excitement and the lieutenant junior-grade's embarrassment seemed inappropriate to what had occurred.

"Very well," the latter finally, incongruously ground out of himself. "Instruct the guards not to let the other two out of their sight for a minute during the rest of this voyage."

I myself knew that O'Hara was the only one aboard capable of such an act. And even an ignorant man knows that lightning seldom strikes twice in the same place, at least in the same way. I surmised the lieutenant junior-grade's dismay at the fact made him temporarily unable to distinguish between action before it and action after it. This was the one order he had not given, the one place where his system had failed to immunize him, to put him beyond the reach of, fatality. He issued the order now, too late, not so much as a practical measure but as if it were a magic formula for re-establishing him in time.

"I'll give you further instructions when I have communicated with the destroyer," he told the ensign weakly.

The formula had not, would not, work. The irreversible would not be reversed, the irrecoverable recovered. He was beginning to learn what O'Hara had known all along. The value of an act is not an absolute timeless quality of the act. He had given the relevant order too late for it to be relevant, or for its relevance to mean anything. His timing was off. It was the one thing that had betrayed him. A performance that had been otherwise without flaw was discredited by only this single perverse unmanageable element. And it would have to be accounted for. He had failed to anticipate.

"Aye, aye," responded the ensign and bolted down the passageway, his fat buttocks bounding wildly.

So O'Hara, cheated of the command he should have had, for his refusal to exercise the one he did not want had executed upon himself a master's penalty. It had been a command judgment and a command act, by a man who was capable of going down in shipwreck with even so corrupted a hulk of old iron as the *Belle*. It was casuistical, the last exercise possible of his pitiless devotion to form. I could only guess at that point what else it was.

The lieutenant junior-grade made as though to go out on the wing where the signalman was, but could not bring himself to it yet. This thing happened to him against all his intentions and rules, against all his plans and insurances, his knowledge and beliefs, against even his statistics. Yet it affected and implicated him, and he could not for all its untowardness escape it altogether.

I felt more equal to him now, a little superior in fact. O'Hara's suicide, as O'Hara would have known, had put the lieutenant junior-grade in over his head, as the latter's never would have O'Hara. Well, I was thinking, at the restored vibration of the *Belle's* engine which he no longer controlled or felt, O'Hara had died as he had lived, hotly. I had a wayward vision of him lying in his bunk in those raffish shorts, with all his hot blood squirting out of him and all over and around him, so that he lay profoundly in the pride of his remorse and died through his pulses. And perhaps it was best because it was perhaps the one way he would ever be cool and comfortable. He had in this way gone down with his ship, and not altogether of necessity and not altogether in disgrace. Perhaps instead of being as unviable as he himself might once have judged it, it somehow capped his life with a last vestige of dignity.

The result was now something the brisk, trim, doctrinaire lieutenant junior-grade had to cope with, and it was something his mere efficiency and doctrine were not entirely up to. O'Hara in death had established his own long-withheld authority. He would have counted on his suicide giving the lieutenant junior-grade a problem he might eventually accommodate himself to, but could not solve. He may also have counted on this to vindicate the Old Man, whose bridge the lieutenant junior-grade usurped, in the hidden torturing process beyond his control that had hardened his arteries and strangled his brains.

The man who was defeated by demanding too much seemed to me to have won something finally by the act of losing. He seemed to tower over his failure, and over ours. It was like a reprieve, a confounding of doom, the one perfect and impregnable transgression I had almost consciously been needing. It cut through the offensive truth like an act of liberation and rescue, and filled me with inexcusable elation.

"Scum!" exclaimed the lieutenant junior-grade angrily.

I switched my gaze from the destroyer out ahead to examine him. He could not get out of his predicament that way. In my new freedom I was not going to let him off that easily. I wanted to tell him something, and began carefully and devotedly to frame it to myself. I said, they are no worse — or better — than any other similar group of men enmeshed in such a demoralizing series of circumstances, rejected, cut loose from design, with no port of call, left with no more identity than transitory entries on the sailing lists. The thread is hair fine, lieutenant, I argued. They would have given their allegiance even to an imponderable cause, as they had once done, so long as they could see in it for themselves a necessary connection. Life, death — both are bearable in the view of a goal however false or foolish, good or damnable. It is the aimless, the nothing that is insupportable, that maims and kills. When you have no reference to anything or anybody, what does it matter? Who matters? Ours was a revolt, a mutiny by all, by each of us, in the name of human solidarity, against a dissolute authority that trespassed beyond the instinctive limits of decency. If you look at it this way, lieutenant, it becomes possible to understand.

But as I approached the threshold of utterance, I lost the argument I thought I had so clearly formulated, and became unable to re-form to myself the reasons why it had or could have taken place.

"It's unbelievable —" The lieutenant junior-grade was glaring out the open port, through which the made breeze drew blessedly, at the destroyer guiding him. "That's what happens when you have no discipline, no order." He confronted me accusingly across the binnacle, talking to convince himself. "How low," he asked me frigidly, "can you get?"

"Don't accuse me, lieutenant." What I said was nothing like what I had planned to say. "I didn't participate."

The destroyer's wake-light beckoned ahead in the indeterminate twilight, giving me my relative bearing and my course, and a strange warm feeling of apprehension, as it seemed we were leaving for good the safety of an ocean whose impartial beacons were the coursing inextinguishable stars.

183

"Did you take any steps?" The lieutenant junior-grade aimed his question as though he were sighting me in through a pelorus.

His simple audacity, his naïve rectitude based on his unassailable inexperience, annoyed me. He had no sense, no sense whatever, of the perilous balance between conditions and the will. What he had was the artificial advantage of never having deviated from his established code. It had not been sufficient to protect him completely, so that I might have felt sorry for him on account of his own stowaway, for which the code would doubtless take him somewhat to task. But not too sorry, because it would cover him enough.

He faced me squarely and overbearingly. "Did you do anything?"

I made my best effort to shrug away his straightforwardness and folly. "It wouldn't have been any use. What could I do? I had no authority. They would have laughed at me, or —" I reluctantly added, "taken me with them."

Looking me in the eye with the bright intolerant stare of a parrot, he passed, from the confidence of his jurisdiction and with the succinctness of his arbitrary standards, his unarguable judgment.

"If you didn't do anything you are in it as much as the rest."

Then he turned his back on me — it was that elementary — his legs sturdily apart, his feet planted firmly, his arms held staunchly behind him by the fingers of his right hand grasping the wrist of his left — the austere posture of certitude and conviction.

He infuriated me, but I could make no reply. I merely waited for him to submit his awkward message to the destroyer.

24

IT CAME to pass that the rain ceased that afternoon in Sydney, and while the gray dusk piled around me for the last time in the familiar wheelhouse I reflected that I was myself a stowaway on a ghost ship. I glanced once at the dark binnacle. The vacillating unlit compass of my egotism, swinging over others' lives, still had its own homing point to steady on. I retraced my way groping out of the black passages to the main deck, and got ashore.

I went quietly along the quay and turning reviewed the *Belle's* blunt bows and squat superstructure, the masts and crosstrees like gallows, the winches and drums like ancient grinding instruments of torture. In the center of her stony pilothouse with gun turrets on either side above them, the three grim square little ports through which no light reflected from inside or out resembled exactly the high tiny windows of a medieval prison. I shuddered. The disgraceful vessel was a blackened monument to dereliction on all sides, of all kinds and degrees, for all various and contradictory reasons. You planned and organized her, you put her together out of scraps and pieces, and even in the first movement of assembly her dissolution was implicit in the perishable iron.

All over my hands were stained with the dried blood-rust.

Involuntarily I reached into my pocket and touched the papers taking all care of me, assigning me to duties aboard a ship which was a stranger to me and to which I was a stranger, and suddenly I exulted in the power of the mere trivial act and at that moment the *Belle* became just another worn-out, useless old Liberty, that had served her purpose and was ready for the inevitable scrapping. The crowning contradiction was that her disreputable career had made her singular, and singular also the life of every man of her crew, which would otherwise probably have passed innocuously like that of the lieutenant junior-grade.

The lieutenant junior-grade, who must in the normal course of things be a commander by now, had been unquestionably right, but he had no capacity of his own for being either right or wrong, or for facing singlehanded the consequences of being either. And this is no doubt what had made him so insufferable.

I never saw any of them after the inquiry, at which society demanded allegiance to its values and their props even where it had accessory-like withheld both. The Old Man had been hospitalized and remained too ill to appear. The rest fatalistically received their reprimand and uncomfortably, except for Sayles and the steward, accepted the verdict of perfidy passed upon O'Hara's unavailable ghost.

In a way that was beyond them O'Hara had signalized their own untenable state, and they were obscurely glad that he was out of reach. By his death he had not evaded sentence; he appeared instead to have exercised a final control of it, the only control he had left, and the most inviolate in that the sentence could not be retracted, mitigated, commuted, repudiated, or executed by those who could not have understood what it meant. Far from escaping, he imposed, as nothing else he had done could, his own uncompromising terms on life. On death. Society would not lead him captive through the streets. It was the master's duty to be the last to leave the ship — comprised as that is of the ultimate in self-denial which values the lives of all others above your own simply on the arbitrary grounds that they are in your charge, and the ultimate in egotism which automatically implies you are the only one possessing the distinction of this exalted role.

But his suicide was more than a repudiation and immolation — both of which were an essential assertion — of self. It had in it the suggestion of an all-pervading and irremediable dismay. It was an expression of general responsibility for the breakdown of us all, as if in passing and serving his sentence O'Hara paid our penalty and made stick our protest as well as his. The others, being a lesser breed and recognizing that they were a lesser breed, were gratified to let him assume the burden of their fate. If he had been a man who had merely had his finger on his own number, who had not wanted, as Simms had stated it, the damnedest thing of all, he would not have forced the issue, he would have brought them in on schedule. They seemed strangely elevated that he had not done this. I never had the desire to see them again, because I knew their sympathies would wear away under the distracting exigencies of livelihood, along with their sense of what had really happened.

As I walked away to my new billet to engage and to deal with an essential part of myself which I had perhaps not even yet discovered, I wondered how I might face each turn of the future without seeing it altogether as a consequence of these men and this Liberty. With all those conditions and all those individuals, thousands, millions of combinations were possible. Change one aspect of one man or one condition, exert one personality, one will — one will — an immeasurable angle from the way it had taken, and the pattern would have been entirely different. That was the prodigious, unacceptable part of it — that among all the infinite possibilities *this* should have been what transpired. So that what seemed stupefying was not chaos and dissolution but mathematical perfection —

like the precariously, pointlessly balanced Stillson wrench —
the referenceless symmetry of a million iotas, a shift in any
of which would have realized one of a billion other potentiali-
ties, which had caused instead by an arresting algebra just,
precisely, irretrievably this!

Years later in a flash or a shadow was revealed to me,
stowed away in my imagination, the fact that something
other than what did happen could have happened, had
happened many times over and would again happen, if only
in my mind. So in effect I have told two stories, the one
which did not take place redeeming the one which did.